A Dream of Sadler's Wells

Lorna Hill wrote her first stories in an exercise book after watching Pavlova dance in Newcastle. Her daughter Vicki, aged ten, discovered one of these stories and was so delighted by it that Lorna Hill wrote several more and soon they were published. Vicki trained as a ballet dancer at Sadler's Wells and from her letters Mrs Hill was able to glean the knowledge which forms the background for the 'Wells' stories.

A Dream of Sadler's Wells tells of Veronica, whose great ambition is to dance in *The Sleeping Beauty* at Covent Garden. After numerous setbacks she finally gains admission to the Royal Ballet School at Sadler's Wells.

Veronica at the Wells, *No Castanets at the Wells* and *Masquerade at the Wells* are also published in Piccolo.

D1355619

Lorna Hill

A Dream of Sadler's Wells

illustrated by Kathleen Whapham

Piccolo Pan Books

First published 1950 by Evans Brothers Ltd
This edition published 1972 by Pan Books Ltd
Cavaye Place, London SW10 9PG
2nd printing 1976
Copyright Lorna Hill 1950
ISBN 0 330 02898 7
Printed in Great Britain by
Richard Clay (The Chaucer Press) Ltd, Bungay, Suffolk

For my daughter Vicki,
who was once a pupil at the
Sadler's Wells School of Ballet

AUTHOR'S NOTE

I should like to express my thanks to Dame Ninette de Valois for reading the manuscript of this book, which is so closely concerned with Sadler's Wells.

Contents

Part One

The Dream

Chapter 1

The Flying Scotsman

ONE of the blackest days of my life was on a certain Tuesday at the end of July. Not that you could call the day itself black. In fact the sky was so blue, the sun streaming through the carriage windows so hot, the fields so green where they were not gilded all over with buttercups, that all these bright things only seemed to make my gloom all the deeper.

The very train, hurling itself into tunnels with a triumphant shriek, snorting over bridges, snaking round corners, its back end curling after it like an outsize in caterpillars, racketing through unimportant stations with a disdainful hiss, and finally grinding on its brakes at Darlington – the very train seemed to say: 'Well, here you are, you Sassenachs! Not much of a place, is it? Take it or leave it – all the same to me! I'm a Scot myself, of course. Haven't any time for these English towns. Take your seats, please! ...'

'Oh, dear!' I said under my breath. It was awful having to leave dear old London at a moment's notice; to say goodbye for ever to the warm and noisy Underground with its escalators crowded with chattering, laughing people, all being carried up or down as if on a magic carpet; the bus drivers with their friendly Cockney voices; the well-known statues and monuments – Nelson on his column, Eros in Piccadilly Circus, Peter Pan in Kensington Gardens. Then there was the Zoo. My heart ached to think of the Zoo with my own favourite little monkey, Jacko, in it. For one thing I was pretty sure nobody would think of taking him liquorice all-sorts – the little round ones covered with comfits that he loved so much. It was sweet to watch him lick off the coloured sweets and stick the liquorice on the bars of his cage like chewing gum! All this was bad enough, but added to the sum total of my misery was the awful thought of the Unknown Relations waiting to pounce on me at the other end of my long journey.

The relations lived in the cold and unfriendly North of England, where people spoke practically a foreign language. At least Mrs Crapper, who'd looked after me since Daddy died, said so, and *she* ought to know because her sister is married to a man who lives in Newcastle. Mrs Crapper said that people called you 'hinny' – even in the shops – instead of 'modom' like they do in London. 'Hinny' was a word I'd never heard before, and I didn't like the sound of it very much. Mrs Crapper also said that if you were a man, everyone called you 'Geordie', even if your name wasn't George at all, but Harry or Archibald.

The relations were rich, and they lived in a large, grey unfriendly house. I'd never seen the house, as a matter of fact, but I felt quite sure that it *was* grey and unfriendly. The relations had three cars – a shooting-brake for Uncle John, the little Morris for Aunt June to go shopping in, and the Rolls. The latter was driven by a chauffeur because it had to be treated with care, being terribly valuable. Fiona, one of the Unknown Cousins, had told me this when she'd spent a week in London with Aunt June ages ago. They'd come to see Daddy and me, and I remembered vaguely that Fiona was fair, very pretty, and beautifully dressed. I rather wished now that I'd taken more notice of her, but at the time she hadn't seemed terribly important.

I sighed again. The carriage was a non-smoker, but the occupants – two men and three women – were all now smoking like chimneys. They had politely asked each other's permission to do so, but they hadn't asked mine. I expect they thought that I was only a child – not old enough to matter, or to have any feelings. I wondered what would happen if I were to be sick in their dignified midst! I decided that it would jolly well serve them right for being so thoughtless and selfish. On the other hand it's not a very nice feeling being sick, so I hastily got up and dashed out into the corridor, nearly colliding with a fellow traveller coming in the opposite direction.

'S-sorry!' I gasped. 'But I just *had* to get out of there quickly. In another minute I'd have been sick. All that smoke! ...'

'Golly! ...' The voice was a boy's voice. It sounded a bit anxious, due I expect to my explanation about the hurry.

'Oh, it's all right,' I assured him, gulping down breaths of fresh air from the open corridor window beside me, 'I don't feel a bit sick now. It was just the smoke. They were *all* smoking,' I added reproachfully, 'even the women.'

'Women do smoke nowadays, you know,' said the boy pleasantly.

I glanced at him suspiciously, but he didn't look as though he were being sarcastic.

'It was a *non-smoker*,' I told him severely.

He looked at me with raised eyebrows.

'I'm afraid you're what you might call a bit temperamental, my child.'

'Temperamental? How dare you! I'm not the least bit temperamental! The carriage was absolutely *full* of smoke. And I'm not your child!'

13

'Naughty, naughty!' said the boy, with more than a hint of laughter in his voice.

'Do you mean them – or me?' I demanded stiffly.

'Take your choice,' said the boy easily. 'In other words – if the cap fits, wear it! Personally I like a bit of a fug.'

'Well, I *don't*,' I said emphatically. 'Not in a small space like a railway carriage, anyway. And if you like it, why are you out here? Isn't there a seat for you? I'm sure you can have mine?'

'Now don't go getting your rag out, or I shan't give you a sandwich,' said the boy. 'I've got some lemonade, too! When I travel I always carry my own canteen with me. You can't trust the meals on these trains. Too expensive, anyway.'

I hesitated, torn between pride and loneliness. Finally loneliness won.

'Have you come far?' I asked him as he led the way to the end of the corridor.

'No – got in at Darlington. I've been staying there with an aunt on my way home from school. We broke up nearly a week ago.'

'I've come from London,' I said importantly. 'I'm going to Newcastle to live with my cousins. You see, my aunt and uncle promised Daddy they'd look after me.'

'London?' said my companion with interest. 'All the way from London! You must find things very different here, poor child – savage and so on?'

I glanced out of the window at the neat little fields flying past.

'No – not very. In fact it's really just the same, only a bit cleaner and colder looking. But I don't believe you meant that seriously. You were having me on.'

'*Me* have you on?' echoed the boy. 'Oh, never, dear lady! Noel Coward, by the way,' he added. 'I mean the "dear lady" touch. Great favourite of mine, Coward.'

'Oh, is he?' I said eagerly. 'I like him awfully too – as an actor, I mean. I like his plays and films as well. The film of *Brief Encounter* was grand.'

'Yes, wasn't it?' agreed the boy. 'Especially the music. I went three times just to hear the Rachmaninoff Concerto. It was Eileen Joyce playing, you know, with the London Symphony Orchestra.'

'Was it?' I said. 'I didn't know that, but I loved it all the same. You like music?'

The boy stared out of the window.

'As I won't be seeing you again, I'll make a confession. Yes, I do like music. I like it so much I'm going to make it my career. Nobody knows that yet, of course. At the present moment my father thinks I'm going to be – well, something quite different.'

I drew a deep breath.

'I'll make a confession too then,' I said. 'I'm going to be a dancer. How I don't quite know, but I intend to do it somehow.'

'You'll have to get going, won't you?' observed my companion. 'You have to begin young, haven't you – in the cradle practically.'

'I've already begun,' I told him. 'I began when I was ten which is the right age. I'm fourteen now. The question is how I'm to go on learning, now I've got to live in this place.' I stared disconsolately out of the window at the cathedral towers of a city we were passing.

'Durham,' said the boy, following my gaze. 'I see – well, I expect you'll manage it somehow, if you've made up your mind.'

'I expect I shall,' I said, 'or die in the attempt! One couldn't have four years under Madame, and then give it up – just like that.' I snapped my fingers.

'Madame who?' queried the boy.

'Oh, we just call her "Madame". Her real name's a bit weird, you see. It's Madame Violetta Wakulski-Viret. She's part Italian, part French, and part goodness knows what! Added to that she married a Russian – hence the "Wakulski". She speaks every language under the sun. If she's pleased with you, which isn't very often, she coos at you in French or broken English. If she's frightfully annoyed, she shouts at you in Russian or Italian, and if she's talking business, she does it in German. It's useful because you know what sort of a mood she's in by the language she uses!'

The boy whistled.

'She sounds a queer customer!'

'Oh, yes,' I said. 'All the best teachers seem to be queer. I once gatecrashed into the Wells School at Colet Gardens—'

'The Wells?—'

'Sadler's Wells,' I explained. 'Everyone who goes there just calls it the Wells, you know. Well, as I say, a girl who's a student there – she lived on the floor above us – smuggled me in. I wore her grey tunic and pink tights and my hair screwed up as if I were going to have a bath – just like all the other students. It was at the beginning of term so I expect they thought I was a new girl. Anyway, I crept up into the balcony above the Baylis Hall and watched one of the classes, and no one knew I was there.' I shuddered. 'Gosh! I'd hate to think what would have happened to me if I'd been found out – they hate you to watch their classes! The master who was taking the class was frightfully temperamental. He shouted, and stormed, and banged with his stick on the *barre* – I'd have been scared to death – but it was obvious that they all thought the world of him. Oh, he was grand!'

'U-m,' said the boy dubiously. 'Sounds a rum go to me! And you really want to study there?'

'At the Wells? I should just say I do! I shouldn't care how they shouted at me. Of course, I want to get into the Sadler's

I'd work and work and watch the principals

Wells Ballet – everyone does – everyone who dances, I mean. But you've got to be terribly good, even to get into the school; I'd be in the very back row of the bottom class. Then, if I got into the Company, of course I'd be in the very back row of the *corps de ballet*; everyone is when they begin. But I'd work and work and watch the principals, and then one day *I'd* be the Lilac Fairy in *The Sleeping Beauty*. I know *exactly* how I should do it. Not brilliant at all – just dreamily, like lilac on a cool summer evening in the moonlight with the dew falling.'

'Wouldn't you like to dance the Finger Variation – the Breadcrumb Fairy?' said the boy quite seriously, so seriously that I stared at him in astonishment. 'They call her the Fairy of the Golden Vine now, I believe – a great mistake in my opinion. I liked the old name much better.'

'Look here,' I said. 'You seem to know an awful lot about ballet?'

'Matter of fact I'm dead keen on it,' said the boy. 'Another confession!' Then his face changed as if he thought he'd been serious too long. 'I once went to see Helpmann in *Hamlet*. Grand!' He went down on one knee on the floor and gave a vigorous imitation of Hamlet in his death agony. I couldn't help laughing.

'I thought you said something about sandwiches?'

He got up hastily.

'Oh, yes – here they are. Ham and tongue. Aunt Alice's best! And you can have a drop of my lemonade as well if you like. I'll let you have a pull at the bottle first. Always the little gentleman!'

I accepted the bottle and took a long refreshing drink. Really, he was the queerest boy I'd ever seen. As he munched his sandwich I stared at him curiously.

He looked about fifteen, and he was very thin, with what you would call an 'interesting' face, rather than good-looking. His eyes were blue – not light blue, but dark, and sparkling, and slightly on the slant. His hands fascinated me. They were strong, and slender, and very sensitive, and he moved them about continually as he talked. I'd never seen anyone with hands like that. In fact I'd never seen anyone like him at all. I wondered what his name was.

'Go on,' he said, between bites. 'I see it coming. Spit it out!'

'I don't know what you mean.'

'Oh yes, you do. You were going to ask my name.'

I blushed.

'Well, what if I was?'

'Nothing – only I'm not telling you, that's all! I've told you quite enough without unfolding the folly of my name.'

'Oh, then it's a queer name?' I teased.

'Well, it's not the sort of name a fellow likes to take to school with him. Otherwise it's original and it'll be a great asset to me in my musical career. By the way, you said you were going to live with relations up north. Father in the Army?'

'No,' I said stonily. 'A clergyman.'

'Oh—' There was a note of mock solemnity in my companion's voice. He took a pair of compasses out of his pocket, clipped them on his nose, folded his hands, and gazed at me parsonically over the top of them. 'Oh – parson's daughter?'

'I *was* a parson's daughter,' I said, stifling a sob, and I suppose I still am – in a way. You see – Daddy died not so long ago.'

The teasing look faded from the boy's face as if it had been wiped away with a sponge. He took off the mock spectacles, dropped them into his pocket, and put his arm round me.

'Oh, bad luck! Sorry and all that. I had no idea.'

'Of course you hadn't,' I said, struggling with my tears. 'But it's so *awful*. If only I could have stayed in London, Mrs Crapper would have looked after me and I could have gone on dancing. But of course it was impossible – at least Uncle John said it was when he came to settle things a few weeks ago. He was horrified at the very idea of Mrs Crapper, though I can't think why. Uncle John isn't what you might call very understanding. Anyway, I couldn't get him to see that ballet is a perfectly serious career, and not just showing off. Then there was the question of school. You see, when Daddy was alive he taught me himself.'

'Have another sandwich,' my companion said, looking the other way while I dried my eyes. 'I'm most awfully sorry. I wouldn't have joked if I'd known.'

'Of course you wouldn't,' I said. In spite of his queerness I liked him awfully. He seemed my only friend in a strange and alien world. 'And thank you for the lemonade and the sandwiches. I think I'd better go back to my compartment now. We're just coming to Newcastle, aren't we? Mrs Crapper said it was after Durham.'

'Good Lord, yes!' exclaimed the boy. 'I'd better be getting back to mine, too. It's right at the other end of the train and all my traps are in it. S'long! I hope you manage the dancing lessons all right. By the way, are the relations meeting you?'

'Oh, yes,' I answered. 'I'll manage somehow – the dancing, I mean. And thank you again.'

I dashed back along the swaying corridor to my compartment and collected my things at lightning speed. Then, after I had straightened my beret, I put on my gloves and braved myself to face my dismal future.

Chapter 2

The Unknown Relations

They were all there – all of them, that is, except Uncle John, and I expect he was still at his office in Nun Street. Uncle John is what Fiona calls a 'shipping magnate'. I'm not quite sure what the 'magnate' means but when I asked Mrs Crapper she said it was a thing you picked up pins with when you were dressmaking. I can't imagine Uncle John picking up pins, even with a magnate, so I expect it's something different when you use it with ships. As we rolled out from under the dark station portico in the large shining car, I stared at them curiously, and I must say that if it was rude of me to stare, they were rude too – even Aunt June. I think she stared even harder than Fiona and Caroline.

'Well, Veronica,' she said at length, holding on to the tassel that hung down beside the window, as if she were strap-hanging in a bus instead of reclining in a palatial car. 'You've changed a great deal since I saw you last. You're not at all like your mother.'

I knew at once that this wasn't a compliment because I'd been told so many times that my mother was beautiful. A pang shot through me. When you get to be as old as fourteen, you like to be thought pretty, especially when the people you're with are pretty, and there was no doubt about it – Fiona and Caroline were both lovely. At least Fiona was beautiful now, and you could see that Caroline would be too when she was older and had slimmed down a bit.

'I think I'd rather be like Daddy,' I said stoutly, crushing

21

down the pang. I felt it was hard luck that no one should want to be like him. 'You see I can't remember Mummy, but Daddy—' Tears came into my eyes.

'No, of course not,' Aunt June said in a matter-of-fact tone of voice, adding as an afterthought: 'Poor child!'

'Are you older than me, or younger?' Fiona asked as the car purred up Westgate Hill which leads out of Newcastle.

'I'm fourteen. I was fourteen last May.'

'I'm fourteen and a half,' Fiona informed me in a superior tone of voice.

'Fourteen last April,' corrected Caroline. 'That's not fourteen and a half. It isn't even fourteen and a quarter. You're only a month older than Veronica.'

Fiona didn't look very pleased at this interruption.

'I'm eleven,' Caroline went on, quite unperturbed, 'but I'm so big that everyone thinks I'm as old as Fiona.'

'No, they don't,' Fiona said flatly. 'You aren't nearly as big as me, Caroline, so don't tell stories – unless it's big *round*.'

This silenced Caroline for a bit.

'What I can't understand,' went on Aunt June, 'is the fact of your Mrs Cripps—'

'Crapper,' I corrected firmly.

'Crapper, then. I simply can't understand the woman allowing you to travel all that way by yourself – and not even in a first-class compartment. Most reprehensible!'

I didn't know what 'reprehensible' meant, but I gathered that it wasn't anything nice, and I wasn't going to have poor Mrs Crapper blamed.

'Oh, but Mrs Crapper would never even *think* of first class,' I said. 'And anyway, I go about everywhere at home by myself. On the tops of the buses – in the Tube—'

'The *what* did you say?' interrupted Caroline.

'The Tube – underground train, you know,' I repeated. 'Don't they have a Tube in Newcastle?'

22

Fiona gave a peal of laughter.

'Gosh, no! Wait till you've *seen* Newcastle. It's just like a village compared with London. Caroline's never been to London. *I* have – several times.'

'Twice,' Caroline stated flatly. 'And once was only a week-end on the way to somewhere else.'

'Well, anyway, I've been there,' Fiona argued. 'And I've been on top of a bus, *and* in the Tube, and on the escalators, and I've seen the Houses of Parliament, and the Tower, and Marble Arch, and when I came back here everything looked terribly queer – as if it had shrunk, and all in slow motion.' She glared at me in anything but friendly fashion as if it were my fault that her sister persisted in taking her down a peg.

I glanced at Aunt June, wondering what she thought about all these heated arguments going on over her dead body, so to speak. But she didn't seem at all perturbed. As a matter of fact I don't think she was listening. Later on I discovered that whatever Fiona and Caroline said and did when their mother was there, they were ten times worse when she wasn't!

We had left the suburbs by this time, and the car was speeding along white roads, bordered at first by neat little hedges and railings, then by taller hedges and less neat railings. Finally the hedges and railings were replaced by low stone walls or sunk ditches filled with bracken and meadowsweet. Sometimes the road wound through shadowy plantations of fir and larch, the overhanging branches of the trees brushing the car roof as we passed. Rabbits ran out, stared at us, then disappeared with a flicker of their white tails. Pheasants and partridges – Caroline told me their names – rose out of the green depths of the woods with a metallic whirring sound, as if they were made of clockwork. It was all very cool, and peaceful, and North Country.

I sighed. It was so unlike my beloved London.

Presently we turned sharply to the right, and the car

stopped outside tall wrought-iron gates, beside which stood a cottage with glittering, diamond-paned windows under the eaves, and queer twisted chimneys. I expected the little green door to open and a rosy-cheeked gardener's wife to swing open the gates for us as in *Little Lord Fauntleroy*, but the door remained shut, and Perkins, Aunt June's chauffeur, began to get out of the car to open the gates himself.

I sprang up.

'I'll do it, shall I? ... It's all right, Perkins!' I yelled through the glass partition, nearly tripping over the luxurious fur rug that covered the floor. But to my surprise he didn't stop getting out. Instead Fiona stared at me, and Aunt June gripped me firmly by the arm.

'Sit down, dear. Perkins will see to it.'

'Oh, but poor man!' I exclaimed. 'It's awful when you're driving a car and have to open things yourself; it takes three times as long, and wastes ever so much petrol. Mr Salmon – he's a friend of Daddy's, and he has a frightfully old car – well, if he stopped to open gates, he'd simply never get the car to start again. So he always takes me with him. I mean, he always *took* me with him,' I corrected hastily, remembering that all these things were now in the past. 'So you see I'm frightfully good at gates, I know all their little tricks, the ones you have to lift, and the ones—'

'How amusing!' Aunt June said, cutting me short, and I had a feeling that she wasn't a bit amused really. 'Perkins opens the gates for us here.'

By now we had come to the front door, and this time I didn't try to jump out first and give them a helping hand. I waited for Perkins to walk round and open the car door, which he did in a very dignified manner.

'You'd better take Veronica upstairs,' Aunt June said when we were in the hall. By the way, the latter was large and square and panelled like a room, and there was a fireplace at each end. There were great blue jars, filled with pink and blue lupins, standing at each side of the shallow oak staircase leading to a gallery above. There were soft carpets which went right up to the panelling, and covered all the passages that led off from the hall – quite unlike the vestibule of Mrs Crapper's house which had a cement floor and smelt of disinfectant. 'She's to sleep in your room, you know, Fiona,' Aunt June was saying.

'Oh, all right, Mummy,' Fiona said obediently, but I saw her screw up her face behind Aunt June's back in a way that made me feel she didn't like the arrangement any too well. 'Come on, Veronica.'

'By the way, Veronica,' Caroline said when we had reached Fiona's bedroom and had taken off our coats and brushed our hair, 'you mustn't try to open gates and things for Perkins when Mummy's there. She'll be frightfully annoyed. I hope you don't mind my telling you.'

'All right,' I said slowly. 'Thanks for the hint. It did seem awful though – three of us, all with arms and legs and things, and poor Perkins—'

'Yes, I know, and when we're in the car with him by ourselves we always do it. But Mummy thinks it's *infra dig*.'

'So it is,' snapped Fiona. 'I think Perkins ought to do it. After all, he's a chauffeur, isn't he? It's what he's paid for.'

'Sebastian doesn't think like that,' Caroline retorted. 'Sebastian says when you can do a thing for yourself, you jolly well ought to do it. He says he's never going to have a chauffeur; he says people who have chauffeurs lose the use of their legs.'

'He's having you on!' Fiona said scornfully. 'You know what Sebastian is; you can never believe a word he says. Anyway, he isn't the least bit likely ever to have a chauffeur. Uncle Adrian's frightfully hard up.'

'You remember the other day when we were waiting for Mummy at the Women's Institute meeting?' Caroline said, stealing a sidelong look at Fiona from under her eyelashes. 'Well, I heard Mrs Musgrave say we were *nouveau riche*. What do you suppose she meant?'

'How do I know!' snapped Fiona. 'I don't care, either – revolting old hag! Who's Mrs Musgrave, anyway?'

'Well, she's frightfully ancient and historic, isn't she?' persisted Caroline. 'I mean, her family is. They come in *Young Lochinvar* ... "Fosters, Fenwicks, and Musgraves; they rode and they ran".'

'She can come in "The boy stood on the burning deck" and ride as hard as John Gilpin for all I care!' declared Fiona. 'She's an interfering old hag all the same.' Then she turned to me: 'I'm sure I don't know where you're going to put your clothes – mine take up all the room in the wardrobe.'

'Trixie said she was going to bring in more hangers,' put in Caroline promptly. I gathered that Trixie had been Caroline and Fiona's 'nannie' when they were children. 'You'd better move your things along, Fiona – there's loads of room.'

'There isn't loads of room,' Fiona grumbled. 'I hate having my things all squashed together.' She moved a couple of dresses along the rail and grudgingly showed me the space. 'You can have that bit if you like. I hope you haven't got masses of clothes.'

I'd have laughed if I hadn't felt so near crying.

'Masses of clothes? Why, I've hardly got any. I can get all my things in there – easily.'

'Oh, well, that's a good thing anyway. I don't see why it's always me who has to have someone stuffed into their room.'

'Mine isn't big enough for two beds,' Caroline said; 'You know that, Fiona. If it was, Veronica could share mine. I'd like her to.'

A glow went through me at her friendly words.

'I don't mind about a bed,' I said emphatically. 'I'd *like* to sleep in your room, Caroline. I'll sleep on the floor. I've often

26

done it at home when Daddy had a guest. We hadn't a spare room.'

'Don't be stupid!' exclaimed Fiona impatiently. 'Mummy would have a fit.' Then she added: 'I should have thought you'd have had loads of room in the vicarage. Our vicar's always saying that vicarages are miles and miles too big for any modern person to live in.'

'Our house wasn't a real vicarage, you see,' I explained. 'The real vicarage was quite a nice house, but it was bombed in the blitz on London, and the new one hasn't been built yet. So the vicarage was just an orinary flat – a bit of a big house. It belonged to Mrs Crapper and she lived on the ground floor, and let off the rest to all sorts of people. That's how she made a living. You see, Mrs Crapper's husband was what Daddy called a waster; he just walked out and left her high and dry, and she didn't know where he was, so the apartment house was a good idea. The basement was the parish hall.'

'How ghastly!' commented Fiona.

'It wasn't ghastly at all,' I flashed, an awful pang of home-sickness shooting through me. 'I loved every minute of it. Two girls who were going to be dancers had rooms over ours. One was going in for musical comedy – tap dancing and things – and the other was a ballet student. She was at the Wells – Sadler's Wells School I mean. I used to watch them practising and sometimes I practised with them. Then on the very top floor – as a matter of fact it was really one huge attic with a perfectly enormous skylight – there was Jonathan. I should say Mr Rosenbaum, but everybody called him Jonathan. He was an artist, and he used to let me paint on the backs of his canvases – the ones he said he couldn't stand at any price. As a matter of fact he painted me last year . . .'

'Painted you?' Fiona broke in scornfully. 'Whatever for? Were you supposed to be a gipsy, or a child of the gutter, or what?'

There was an awful silence. I turned scarlet.

'It isn't only people with golden hair and pink faces who get painted.' I burst out hotly. As a matter of fact artists prefer the other kind. Jonathan said I had a very striking face . . .'

I was speaking to the empty air. Fiona had fled.

'I'm frightfully sorry,' Caroline muttered, staring after her sister with puckered brow. 'That was awful – what she said. You mustn't take any notice of her, Veronica. She didn't mean it – really she didn't. She's jealous, that's all.'

'Jealous?' I echoed. 'What on earth of?'

'Of you.'

'Of me? Oh, but . . .' Words failed me. The bare idea of Fiona, with her golden hair and beautiful face, being jealous of me sounded just ridiculous.

'She's jealous because you lived in London,' explained Caroline. 'Fiona thinks it's marvellous to live in London.'

'Oh well – if that's all that's the matter with her, I expect she'll get over it,' I said slowly.

'Sebastian says she's spoilt,' went on Caroline. 'Sebastian spends most of his time squashing Fiona.'

'Look here, who *is* Sebastian?' I demanded. 'You're always talking about him. Is he a gardener or someone?'

'The gardener?' laughed Caroline. 'Gracious, no! He's our cousin. His father is Daddy's brother, only Uncle Adrian, Sebastian's father, is Sir Adrian Scott. He's the eldest son, so he came into the estate; that's why they're as poor as church mice. Estates do seem to eat away fortunes, don't they? Daddy was the youngest son, and a plain "mister", so he went into trade. We were very poor at first, though Fiona won't admit it, but now Daddy's got oodles of money. That's what Mrs Musgrave meant when she called us New Rich. I looked it up in the French dictionary. I expect she'd call Uncle Adrian and Sebastian New Poor!'

'How old is Sebastian?' I asked, getting back to the point.

'He's fifteen – just a year older than Fiona,' Caroline said. 'That's what annoys her. She can't put on airs with him.'

'Do you like him?' I asked.

'Frightfully,' confessed Caroline. 'Everything's exciting where Sebastian is. He's a marvellous rider and he swims like a fish.'

'You mean he's clever?'

Caroline looked blank.

'Clever? You mean at lessons? Haven't an earthly. I expect he is, though – he's going to be a lawyer. I can't imagine Sebastian *not* being able to do anything – even Latin irregulars or algebra ... Oh, there's the gong! That means tea's ready; we have it in the schoolroom now. Fiona gets frightfully annoyed if you call it the nursery.'

Chapter 3

The Fate of a Frock

It's queer how, when you stay at a strange place, an hour can seem as long as a week – even when it's the holidays which usually go like a flash, however hard you try to spin them out. By half past seven I felt as if I had been at Bracken Hall for at least a year. Not a very pleasant year, either!

'We don't go down for dinner,' Caroline explained. 'We have supper up here in the nursery – I mean the schoolroom,' she added hastily, seeing Fiona's disapproving eyes upon her.

I sighed. To tell you the truth, I was getting heartily sick of the schoolroom. To my mind it was a terribly uninteresting place. There were two bookcases: one was full of school textbooks, like *Longman's Geography, Elementary Algebra,* and *Caesar's Gallic Wars.* The latter made me shudder even to look at them! The other was crammed with school stories: *Winifred Wins Through, The Head Girl of Saint Anthony's, Fenella of the Fifth,* and so on. Nothing decent like a book about ballet, or even *The Children's Encyclopedia.* There were no decent pictures on the walls, either – just colour-prints of animals and fairies; not an original among them.

'What time do we have to go to bed?' I asked as we began on the tomato soup and chocolate blancmange that was set out on the nursery table. I knew quite well by now that there would be a set time for going to bed, and that it would be early. Not a bit like home, where I went to bed any time I liked.

'You and Miss Caroline go at eight,' Trixie said. 'Miss Fiona goes at half past. The mistress thinks you need a lot of sleep and good wholesome food, Miss Veronica, you being so pale and thin. We must make you a big bonny girl like Miss Caroline, mustn't we? Now eat up every scrap of that nice blancmange, and I've got a big glass of fresh milk for you before you go to bed.'

'Sounds like fattening up a pig for market!' Fiona put in scoffingly.

'Now none of your rude remarks, Miss Fiona,' Trixie said severely, looking at Fiona with disapproval. 'You must be kind to your little cousin and make her feel at home.'

I'm afraid I wasn't nearly as grateful to Trixie as I ought to have been. For one thing, I didn't want to be big and fat – not for dancing. Whoever heard of a big, fat, bouncing *ballerina*! Still, she meant to be kind, so I smiled at her when she brought the milk and said 'thank you' in what I hoped was a grateful-sounding voice. As I said before, Trixie had been the Scotts' 'nannie' when they were little. Now she was – well, it was really hard to say exactly what she was. Even Fiona found it difficult to explain.

'She looks after us in the hols, and sees to our clothes and things,' she said vaguely when Trixie was out of the room. 'When we're at school she helps Mummy with the house. Really I think Mummy just keeps her out of charity. She does hardly anything.'

'Oh, I don't know,' put in Caroline. 'Trixie's always busy, and I've heard Mummy say she's as good as a housekeeper any day.'

'You'd better have your bath first tonight, Miss Veronica,' Trixie said when she returned. 'You'll be tired after your long journey. And don't be too long over it. Remember there's Miss Caroline after you.'

'Oh, yes – I'm to use Mummy's bathroom, Trixie,' Fiona

said loftily. 'I shall use loads of bath salts and talcum powder.'

'Not Mummy's, I hope?' Caroline put in.

'No, it's my own. Aunt Millicent gave it me at Christmas, and it seemed a waste to use it in the mouldy nurs— schoolroom bathroom.'

After we'd finished our supper, which was a lot nicer than it looked I'm bound to admit, and I'd collected up my dressing-gown and slippers, I trekked off to the bathroom, Caroline close on my heels.

'You can't lock the door,' she explained. 'Fiona used to go in there for her bath and stay in simply *ages* – just to annoy Trixie. So the key was taken away.'

'Well, I don't mind,' I assured her. 'If people like to barge in when I'm having my bath, it's OK with me!'

As a matter of fact Fiona did barge in, without even troubling to knock. She had on a lovely, pale blue, quilted silk dressing-gown, that exactly matched her eyes, and blue satin slippers with swansdown round the tops of them.

'I'm just finished,' I said, tying my girdle and spreading out the towels to dry on the airer. I was about to pull the bathplug so that I could wipe out the bath when Fiona stopped me.

'You needn't bother to do all that,' she declared. 'Trixie will do it. That's what she's there for. By the way, you won't need *that* tomorrow' – she poked with her finger at the frock I'd been wearing, and which I now held in my arms on top of my other things. 'I'll lend you some shorts and a blouse until your trunk comes from the station.'

I stared at the dress in my arms.

'What's the matter with my frock?' I demanded.

'Well, it's on the dirty side, you must admit,' Fiona stated. 'Quite frankly, it looks like something the cat's brought in.'

Another awful flood of homesickness swept over me. The frock meant a bit of home to me, though Fiona was quite right

– it was certainly crushed and not very clean.

'Mrs Crapper gave it to me,' I explained. 'She got the material at a sale, and it was a terrific bargain – only eightpence ha'penny a yard. She made it for my birthday, and she took no end of trouble over it. So, if you don't mind, Fiona, I'll just go on wearing it until my own things come. Then I can wash and iron it. Thank you for offering to lend me your shorts all the same.'

'That's all very well, but what about *us*?' demanded Fiona. 'What about Caroline and me having to go about with you looking like the dog's dinner, and everyone *knowing* we're cousins.'

I stared down at the frock and thought of dear Mrs Crapper making it all by hand because she hadn't got a sewing-machine, and, if the stitches *were* rather big and uneven, it was only because her eyes weren't what they had been. I felt I simply couldn't bear Fiona making fun of it.

'I *will* wear it!' I shouted. 'And I'll go on wearing it all the time I'm here if I like. I wouldn't wear your beastly shorts for – for anything!'

'Oh – that's all right,' drawled Fiona off-handedly. Then, without the slightest warning, she snatched the frock from me, and dropped it into the bath.

I leapt forward to rescue it, but her arms were round me. In spite of her fragile and fairylike appearance, she was a lot taller than me, and much stronger than she looked.

'There!' she exclaimed. 'How about wearing it now?' Then she began to laugh. 'Golly – the colour's running!'

It was only too true. The dye of the eightpence ha'penny bargain print was evidently not 'fast'. The bath water was rapidly taking on a lurid hue. It turned pink, then brown, and finally a reddish-purple.

We stared at it, fascinated. An exclamation from the door made us turn. Trixie and Caroline stood there with their mouths open, and the most horrified expressions on their faces.

'It's all right,' Fiona said with a giggle. 'There hasn't been a murder or anything! It's only Veronica's frock. It fell in. It needed a wash, anyway; it was frightfully dirty.'

'Tch! Tch! How careless!' Trixie exclaimed, bustling forward with a great fuss and flurry. 'It needed washing certainly, but *not* in the bath water. Whoever heard of such a thing! Why, the colours aren't "fast"—'

'They aren't, are they?' Fiona said, her giggles increasing.

'It should have been put in salt and water first,' Trixie went on. 'Dear, dear! I'm afraid it's ruined!'

She fished the revolting red and purple mass out of the water, and wrung it out, whereupon streams of red dye covered her hands and flowed into the bath. Finally she draped it over the hot-water cistern to dry.

'Tch! Tch!' she said again. 'I do hope you aren't one of those careless, untidy little girls, Miss Veronica. Such a lot of trouble untidy people make.' She went on reading me a lecture on tidiness while Fiona stood by with a mocking, triumphant expression on her face.

I said nothing, waiting for her to own up, but she didn't. After a few minutes she turned her back upon us, and we heard her singing as she turned on the taps in her mother's bathroom at the other end of the corridor.

'I say,' whispered Caroline when Trixie had finished airing her views on tidiness and had left the room, 'Fiona threw it in there, didn't she? I think it was hateful of her not to tell Trixie, but I couldn't give her away. You do understand, don't you, Veronica?'

'Of course,' I whispered back. 'I wish I were sharing your room, though.'

'I wish you were, too. But cheer up – Fiona will come round. She isn't always such a pig as this. Anyway, Sebastian will be here tomorrow, and he'll keep her in order!'

Sebastian! Sebastian! I was getting quite tired of hearing about him. Probably he'd be horrible like Fiona. Probably his coming would make things worse than they already were.

Chapter 4

Running Away

When Fiona came to bed, I pretended to be asleep. I think she was rather disappointed because she made enough row to wake ten ordinary sleepers. When she found that nothing she did made me so much as wink an eyelid, she got into her own bed near the window and after a while there was silence, so I guessed she had fallen asleep.

I tried to sleep myself, but however hard I tried, I couldn't. Thoughts kept going round and round in my head – thoughts of darling Daddy, gone where I could never see or speak to him any more; of kind Mrs Crapper who'd been a mother to me. It was on Mrs Crapper's shoulder that I had sobbed when someone had sat on my first pair of 'blocked' ballet shoes and squashed them flat; Mrs Crapper who had fastened my ballet frock, and helped pull up my tights when I had entered for my Elementary exam at the Royal Academy of Dancing; she who had consoled me when I'd failed by one mark. Then I thought of Madame kissing me and saying how queer it was that the pupils who would never make dancers, not if they stayed with her for a hundred years, should be left to her, whilst the one she thought might one day succeed should be taken away. She'd offered to let me stay with her for a nominal sum – just enough to pay for my food – so that I could go on with my dancing. Dear Madame – so kind and generous; it had nearly broken my heart to refuse – to tell her that Uncle John had called the idea 'ridiculous nonsense', and forbidden me even to think of it. Finally I thought of Mrs Crapper again and the bargain frock, and the awful mess it had looked when Trixie had fished it out of the bath ... Fiona and her beastly shorts ... Caroline ... tomato soup ... Sebastian ... Sebastian.

I heard the clocks all over the house chiming in different keys – eleven, twelve. After this they seemed to get a bit mixed, so I expect I dropped off to sleep. Anyway, the next thing I remember was the grandfather-clock in the hall striking six.

Suddenly I felt that I could stand it no longer. My mind was made up. I would run away. I had enough money left to get me back to London – by bus, anyhow. I knew it was a great deal cheaper that way than by train because I had heard Mrs Crapper discussing it with a friend. Once I got back to dear old London, I'd be safe. Never, never would I come back here. Anyway, they wouldn't want me if I ran away. I had an uneasy feeling at the back of my mind that there was something disgraceful and cowardly about running away, but I crushed it down firmly. I told myself that Mrs Crapper would understand; that Madame would be overjoyed to have me back; that Jonathan would approve, and that Miriam and Stella, the dancing students in the rooms above ours, would be frightfully pleased to see me. I stole into the bathroom and dressed there for fear of waking Fiona. I picked my frock off the hot-water cistern, and put it on. It looked frightful, but there was nothing else for it. Then, hunching on my blazer, I tiptoed back into the bedroom, shoes in hand, and collected together a few things that I considered necessities – nightie, brush and comb, toothbrush, and a clean hankie. I put them all in my small attaché-case, and on the very top I placed a little parcel wrapped in layers of tissue paper. I couldn't resist the temptation to unfold it and gaze lovingly at what was inside. To any ordinary person the small objects I held so carefully in my hand might have looked like a pair of dirty old pink satin ballet shoes, but to me they were the most romantic shoes in the world. They had belonged to Madame, and she had danced *Lac des Cygnes* and *Les Sylphides* in them. They had danced on Covent Garden stage, and that was enough to make them precious to me. Madame had given them to me with all her love, and I had never been parted from them since. I was certainly not going to leave them behind at Bracken Hall to the tender mercies of Fiona and Aunt June. I wrapped them up tenderly and put them in the case with a sigh.

Swan Lake seemed a thousand miles away from me up here in the savage north of England. And as for *Les Sylphides* – I felt it was indeed a fairy glade which I would never enter!

I took my purse out of the right-hand dressing-table drawer that Fiona had grudgingly said I could use, dropped it into my pocket and gently shut the bedroom door behind me.

Everything was silent in the big house. It was a lovely summer morning, and the early sunlight streamed through the windows with their leaded panes, and flickered through the virginia creeper that framed them, falling upon the floor in pools of warm light. The grandfather-clock in the hall ticked aggressively as I crept softly over the thick carpet towards the front door. The man-in-the-moon on the dial stared at me with a crooked smile, seeing he was just between the quarter and the full, and so was a bit lopsided.

The front door was quite easy to open, and in a very short time I was walking briskly down the drive towards the gate. On my left was a high wall, evidently built to keep out the cold north wind and also curious strangers. It was much too high to look over, let alone climb. Beyond it you could see the tops of the fir woods, and beyond them, rising in misty folds, the high moors of the Border country. Over to the right was a thick shrubbery, with here and there a gap through which you could see gardens and lawns, and, in the distance, parkland with sheep grazing on it.

Presently I came to the gates. They were shut – I had ex-

Swan Lake seemed a thousand miles away from me

pected that – but I certainly hadn't expected them to be locked as they evidently were. I found this out, much to my dismay, when I tried to open them. The question was what to do now. I supposed you had to ask at the little gardener's lodge for the key. I couldn't help wondering what you did if you were on the outside, since the cottage was on the inside. Perhaps you were meant to throw stones at their bedroom window and wake them up that way, but this proceeding seemed a trifle undignified for so stately a place as Bracken Hall!

Of course it was quite easy for me – I was on the inside; all I had to do was to walk up the little garden path, bordered by geranium and blue lobelia, and ring the bell by the side of the green door. But somehow I just couldn't screw up my courage to do it. For one thing it seemed awful to go ringing people's bells – even the gardener's – at half past six in the morning. For another, he might ask awkward questions. Indeed I felt pretty sure he would, seeing me and my attaché-case!

I decided to by-pass the gates. The left side was obviously hopeless because of the wall. I tried turning to the right, only to be met by the wall again. It looked as if it went on and on, right round the estate, even shutting in the sheep!

I came back to the gates. There was nothing for it but to climb them, and I set about doing it. First of all I hooked my case on to a spike at the top of the gate by its handle so that I could reach it afterwards from the other side; then I swung myself up.

All went well until I was just rounding the top. Then my frock hooked itself round a spiky bit of wrought-iron work in that maddening way frocks have when you climb things, and I was caught with one leg over the top of the gate, and the other foot precariously wedged between a wrought-iron waterlily and an outsize in iron spider-webs.

I tried to unhook myself, but couldn't. It was ghastly. I was just thinking that I should have to tear myself free – an awful decision, considering the fact that I hadn't another frock to wear – when a drawling voice below me said:

'I say – if you don't mind my asking – are you breaking in, or breaking out?'

It was so near the truth that I blushed hotly. Screwing round a bit, I looked down, and if it hadn't been for the fact of my frock being so firmly hooked, I'm sure I'd have fallen off that gate with shock, for the owner of the drawling voice – the boy standing outside the door of the little cottage – was none other than my acquaintance of the train. I must say that he looked quite as surprised as I did.

'Gosh!' we said both together in awestruck voices. Then the boy laughed. 'Well, fancy coming across you again! Of all the queer things! So these are the relations you talked about – the Scotts of Bracken Hall. Well, I'm dashed!'

By now I had recovered a little. I said rather crossly: 'I do think you might come and help me, instead of just talking. It's awful being stuck up here.'

'Of course,' said the boy, his mouth taking on its funny one-sided smile. 'I'm only too willing to lend a hand – always ready to oblige a friend, you know. At first I thought you were just taking the air, or admiring the view, or something.'

'Don't be silly!' I said indignantly. 'As if anyone would admire the view on top of a gate as full of spikes as this one is! ... Ouch! ... They stick into you every time you move.'

'Well, people usually go out *through* the gate, not over the top,' teased the boy. 'Still, as I say, I'm only too ready to lend a hand.'

He approached the gate, swung himself up beside me, put an arm round my waist, and heaved me up a few inches. My frock came off the spike and I was free. I began to descend in as dignified a manner as possible, but my rescuer, having jumped down himself, swung me on to the ground beside him. He was really amazingly strong for anyone so slim.

'By the way – as I said before – are you breaking in, or breaking out? I mean, which side of the gate do you want to be on?'

'I want to be on the other side, of course,' I said. 'And I must say I think it's a terribly stupid idea having your gates locked. No one locks *gates* – only doors. A gate would be no use to keep out burglars, even if it *was* locked.'

'No,' agreed the boy. 'But it's quite a good idea for keeping out cows.' Then, seeing the puzzled expression on my face, he added: 'You see, Arkwright – he's the blacksmith in the village – well, he has one or two cows, and he drives them up here every morning into that field over there' – he motioned towards the far side of the road. 'Well, his blessed cows have an annoying little habit of making a beeline for our drive. They scoff all the young wallflowers and so on. Mind you, I don't suppose Arkwright would bother his head about a little thing like that, but a short time ago one of his beasts took a fancy to a yew tree and poisoned itself. Now *that* was quite another matter. There was the dickens of a fuss, and we decided to shut the gates just before going to bed.'

'I can see that,' I said. 'But why go *locking* them? Surely cows can't open gates, and it must be frightfully awkward for visitors—'

'There aren't many visitors after eleven o'clock at night,' answered the boy with a smile. 'And if any do come, there's a bell on the other side that rings into our cottage. As for the cows – no, they can't open gates, though you'd be surprised at some of the things they *can* do – like chewing up your bicycle tyres, and licking the wet paint off the fences. But as a matter of fact, we lock the gates on account of the postman. He has a habit of taking a short cut through the park, and nine times out of ten he leaves the gates open.'

'Oh – I see. Well, how do I get out?' I asked.

The boy put his hand into his pocket, produced a key,

inserted it in the lock, and the gates swung wide.

'We each have one – my father and I,' he told me. 'By the way, I suppose you'll have gathered that I live there?' He nodded towards the pretty cottage. 'Mind if I come along with you for a bit? I'm at a loose end.'

'I'm going pretty fast,' I warned him. 'I mean, I'm not just out for a walk, I'm running away.'

The moment I had said the words I regretted them. After all, if I *was* running away, it was no one's business but my own – least of all the gardener's son, if that was what he was.

'I had a sort of suspicion you were,' the boy remarked. 'If people run away, they usually do it at darkest midnight or crack of dawn. You're a bit late, you know; it's nearly seven o'clock.'

"What about you?' I demanded. 'What are you doing out here so early? You surely can't be digging the garden at this time in the morning?'

'Digging the garden?' echoed the boy. 'Why should I be digging the garden?'

'Helping your father, of course,' I said. 'I expect he's a bit rheumaticky, isn't he? Most gardeners are, Daddy says.' I sighed, remembering the occasion when Daddy had said these words. It had been on one glorious spring day, when we had gone out into the country and had bought some nasturtium plants for Mrs Crapper's window-box at a nursery garden. 'I suppose he finds you a great help – weeding, planting things out, and so on.'

'Oh – er, yes,' said the boy rather doubtfully, I thought.

Then I remembered about his music.

'Oh, but of course – I forgot about your hands. I suppose you won't want to spoil them, messing about with soil,' I said. 'I wonder what your father will say when he finds out you want to be a musician instead of following in his footsteps?'

'Y-es – I wonder,' said my companion still thoughtfully.

Then the queer expression I had come to know so well came back to his face and he added: 'Oh, I expect the old boy will soon get used to the idea of his One-and-Only wielding a conductor's baton instead of a Dutch hoe! More dramatic, what? – if less useful!'

All this time we were walking along the country road.

'As a matter of fact,' said the boy, 'I was just off for a swim in the lake when you hove-to on the horizon. The lake, by the way, is in the park – away behind those trees.' He nodded over his shoulder in the direction of the house. 'And after my swim I was going for a ride. I keep my pony in a field behind the Hall. Well, now I've told you all my business, how about telling me yours? Let's hear for a start why you're running away.'

In spite of myself I told him the bits he didn't know already, trying my hardest to explain about my cousins without telling tales.

'Honestly – I don't think they like me,' I said soberly. 'At least, I'm quite sure Fiona doesn't. Of course it's an awful nuisance for her having me barge in. I take up lots of her wardrobe, and half her dressing-table. I can quite see her point of view, and really I think I'd be much better at home.'

The boy said nothing for quite a long time. Then he remarked: 'I'll tell you what – I'll bet you're just a bit homesick. You'll be OK tomorrow. Why not try it and see?'

I shook my head. 'No. I've quite made up my mind. I couldn't – I simply *couldn't* stay here another minute ... what are you looking like that for?'

'I suppose you realize, my innocent Cockney brat, that there isn't a station in this place?' he said. 'No, not even the Tube round the corner!'

I stood stockstill in the middle of the road. I certainly hadn't reckoned on that. Still—

'Not even a bus, my child,' said the boy, reading my thoughts. 'Not today. Buses only on market days. Market day,

44

Tuesday – this is Wednesday.'

'Well, I shall walk,' I said. 'I shall walk to somewhere where there *is* a bus. After all, it can't be so very far.'

'Can't it?' said the boy. 'My poor child, you don't yet know your Northumberland. Nearest village, Burneyhough – nine miles.'

Dismay surged over me, but I wouldn't admit it.

'I'll walk there if it's a hundred and nine!' I flashed. 'I'll hitch-hike.'

'Quite a good idea,' said the boy, 'if there was anything to hitch to. Distinct lack of traffic on this road, at seven in the morning—'

'*Will* you stop butting in!' I shouted, completely losing my temper. 'I wish you'd go home and hoe your beastly onions, and mind your own business!'

A change came over my companion's face. The bantering look left it, and suddenly his eyes were serious.

'Look here, you can't go through with this, you know. I can't let you – honestly I can't.'

'Can't let me indeed!' I yelled. 'I'd jolly well like to see you try to stop me!'

'Please,' begged the boy. 'Of course I could stop you. You know I could, so do be sensible.'

'And if I won't be sensible?'

'Well, then I suppose we shall have an all-in wrestling match in the middle of the road,' he answered, the fun coming back into his eyes. 'And you'll lose! You'll end up just where you started – on the inside of the gate. You see, boys are always stronger than girls when it comes to a free fight so, lady, have a care!'

'I've told you I won't go back!' I shouted, stamping my foot. 'I can't go back. I can't! I can't! I'd die if I went back!' Tears began to stream down my cheeks.

'Now! Now! Stop this temperamental stuff!' ordered the

45

boy. 'It won't work with me. I know that temperament is just plain temper more often than not, so cut out the dramatics, please!'

'I think you're a h-horrible boy!' I gulped.

'I expect I am,' he agreed. 'But you'll stay – please. I want you to stay – really I do.'

A ray of warmth stole through me at the mere thought of anyone wanting me.

'I suppose I shall have to,' I said slowly. 'I haven't much choice, have I? But I shall still run away later on.'

'OK. We'll discuss that afterwards. It's a dashed good thing you started early on your evil deed! No one need suspect anything. How about coming with me to the lake? Then you can say you went swimming if they ask why you got up so early.'

I hesitated. For one thing I hadn't got a bathing costume or a towel; for another, I felt pretty sure that Aunt June would disapprove frightfully of my going swimming with the gardener's son. Evidently my companion read my thoughts.

'There are loads of swimsuits and things in the boathouse,' he assured me. 'We keep 'em down there.'

I wondered who he meant by 'we', but I didn't like to ask him for fear of seeming inquisitive.

'I – Aunt June—' I began hesitatingly.

'Oh, Aunt June won't mind,' the boy said quickly. 'She knows me. I often swim with Caroline and Fiona in the hols – er – when I'm not hoeing the onions, that is.'

My doubts vanished. After all, if Aunt June didn't mind Caroline and Fiona bathing with the gardener's son, she certainly wouldn't mind *me* doing it. And, after all, he seemed a very superior sort of boy. It occurred to me suddenly that he wasn't a bit like a gardener's son – he didn't speak like one for one thing, and he didn't look like one for another. Although his clothes were old, they were exceedingly well cut, and he wore them with an air.

'I'd love to come,' I said quickly. 'And thank you for asking me.'

'Look here,' said the boy suddenly, as we retraced our steps and walked back through the gates, 'about all those confidences we exchanged yesterday, thinking we were never going to see each other again – all that about our careers and so forth. Let's keep it under our hats, shall we – keep it dark, I mean?'

'Oh, *yes*,' I said emphatically. I certainly wasn't too keen upon Aunt June and Uncle John knowing about my determination to go dancing. 'Yes – let's not say anything to anyone.'

Another glow of warmth stole over me. When you share a secret with someone it gives you a sort of fellow feeling with them. Suddenly everything became much more cheerful. As we strolled across the park, I saw what a perfectly gorgeous place it was. In London the trees had lost their early summer freshness and were becoming tired and dusty. Here they were still so green and glossy that they looked as if they had just been varnished. Not that I loved London any the less; it would always hold first place in my heart, being my home, but I saw how lovely and unspoilt this bit of Northumberland was.

The lake was the most thrilling place I had ever seen. It was fringed by willows on three sides, and on the fourth, where the boathouse was, it had its own little beach of fine silvery sand and pebbles. There was even a tiny island in the middle of the blue water, where, my companion told me, two swans had built their nest in the spring. Now the eggs had been hatched, and the cygnets were quite big.

'Now about swimming costumes,' the boy said when we reached the boathouse. 'Take your choice, lady. We have them in a variety of styles by well-known fashion designers. Here we have Rhapsody in Stripes by Molyneux.' He held up an

47

ancient black and yellow garment. 'Or would you rather have Spotted Peril by Maggy Rouff? Or perhaps a little creation called Darkest Night by Norman Hartnell? As you will perceive it is exquisite in line and material – but of a simplicity *tout à fait ravissante. Mais oui, madame!*'

'You are silly!' I giggled. 'No I don't think I'll have that one,' I added, pushing aside the Spotted Peril. 'It's got mildew. And I *think* the moths have been having a feast on Darkest Night.'

'Moths?' My companion bent closer to examine the costume. '*Mais pardon, madame!* A thousand thousand apologies! Monsieur Hartnell will be *absolument* prostrated to perceive his so beautiful creation *tout à fait* ruined! *Quelle horreur!* It is indeed a tragedy of the first water! *Quel dommage! . . .* That's all the French I know!'

'I think I'll have this one,' I said firmly, picking up the striped garment from the side of the boat where he had flung it. 'I'll make me look like a wasp, but who cares!'

'You're a jolly decent swimmer – for a girl,' said my companion, as we finished a race round the island. 'I believe you're better than either Fiona or Caroline.'

'Am I, do you think?' I said eagerly. Suddenly it seemed terribly important to me to be able to do something really well.

He nodded.

'Yes – but as a matter of fact they're not very good, though Fiona thinks she is! How about landing on the island, and I'll show you where the swans nested. There are moorhens in the reeds as well, though you don't often catch sight of them – they're very shy.'

We spent quite a long time on the island, which was bigger than it looked from the shore. The ground was covered with wild strawberries, and when we were tired of exploring, we sat down in an old duck-punt that was moored among the reeds, and ate masses of them. They had a curious tang – not a bit like garden strawberries; they were the first I'd ever tasted and I loved them.

Suddenly the boy stopped eating, a handful of the tiny scarlet berries halfway to his mouth.

'Gosh! The stable clock!' he exclaimed as a faint, silvery chime reached us from over the water. 'It's a quarter past eight, and breakfast is at half past. I think we'd better be getting back if you don't mind. It won't do to be late; they're dead nuts on punctuality up there' – he nodded in the direction of the house.

'Don't I know it!' I exclaimed, pulling a wry face. 'I expect breakfast will be in the *nursery* – Fiona and Caroline seem to spend all their time in the nursery – I beg its pardon, school-room! I don't believe they *ever* go out!'

'Oh, yes they do – when I'm here, anyway,' the boy told me. 'We have no end of good times, so cheer up! There'll be four of us, now you've come. The more the merrier!'

'You forget – I'm running away, as soon as I've got rid of you,' I told him solemnly.

'If you do, I shall come after you and spank you,' he said, equally solemnly. 'So don't say you haven't been warned!'

But somehow we both knew that I had given up the idea of running away. I didn't even want to now, though how I should put up with Fiona I still didn't know.

For the second time that morning the boy read my thoughts – he seemed rather clever at doing that.

'You needn't worry about Fiona,' he assured me, 'I can manage her all right. She's OK if you keep her down!'

'You said something about a ride?' I said, casting a regretful glance at the rest of the wild strawberries.

'I shall have to put it off till after breakfast. Too late now.' He stood up. 'Race you to the boathouse.'

'By the way,' he said, when we were once more on the main-

49

land, 'hadn't you better dry your hair a bit before you appear at breakfast? It's making a waterfall down your back.'

Suddenly I became acutely conscious, not only of my dripping hair, but of the awful crushed mess that had once been the bargain frock.

'Look here,' I said, looking down at myself ruefully, 'I'm not always in such a mess as this – I mean the frock – but you see, it – it fell into the bath last night, and there was no time to iron it this morning. Besides, the colour ran.'

The boy's blue eyes narrowed.

'I suppose you mean Fiona threw it in?' he said calmly.

I was silent, the colour rushing to my face.

'It's all right – don't look so guilty; you haven't given anything away. You've got an awfully expressive face, but I don't need that to tell me what happened. I know Fiona and her little ways only too well! She's always doing that.'

'What? You mean she *often* throws people's clothes into the bath?'

He laughed.

'Oh, not always in the bath, though she often used to throw her own clothes in when she was a kid – to make poor old Trixie wash them. Once she threw my tennis shoes into the rainwater butt. I'd just whitened them too, and that water barrel was anything but clean, I may tell you. It was full of frog-spawn, soot, slime, not to mention dead woodlice!'

'Gosh!' I exclaimed. The mere thought of anyone daring to take such liberties with the possessions of the boy who stood before me, appalled me. 'What did you do?'

'Fished 'em out,' he said with a short laugh.

'And then?'

'Then ... well, never mind! I thought I'd taught her not to go chucking other people's things about, but evidently I hadn't.'

'Oh, I expect it was just because I was a stranger,' I said.

Somehow Fiona and her queer, unfriendly ways no longer seemed so very important. 'Perhaps she'll stop doing things like that, now she knows I'm here for good.'

'Perhaps,' echoed the boy, but he didn't sound too sure about it.

'Well, goodbye,' I said, as we reached the terrace that stretched all along the south side of the house. Incidentally I noticed that Bracken Hall wasn't the cold, grey house I'd imagined, but low, gracious and mellow with its covering of warm virginia creeper. 'And thank you for being so decent.'

'Don't mention it!' he said, with a mock bow. 'Honoured, I'm sure! Well, so long! I expect I shall see you again today sometime.'

'Oh, I don't suppose so,' I said gloomily. 'As I told you before we seem to spend all our time in the nursery. Besides, there's a horrible boy, called Sebastian, coming – a cousin or something – and I expect we shall have to be polite to him.'

'If you haven't met him, how do you know he's horrible?' demanded my companion.

'He *sounds* horrible,' I declared firmly. 'You don't have to meet some people to know they're horrible. Fiona says she hates Sebastian.'

'Oh – she does, does she?' said the boy. 'And do you always go by what Fiona says?'

'N-no,' I faltered.

'Well, then why not wait and judge Sebastian for yourself. You never know – he might be quite a decent chap.'

'He *might*,' I said, not very hopefully. 'But somehow I don't think so – he's Fiona's cousin. Well, goodbye again. There's the gong! I'll be late for breakfast after all. I must dash!'

Chapter 5

Sebastian

I ran headlong into Fiona who was flying across the hall towards the door I'd just closed.

'Where's Sebastian? Has he gone? Why didn't you tell him to come in and have breakfast with us? I wanted to see him *most* particularly about something, and now – gosh! You are in a mess!'

But I was past being annoyed by anything so trivial as a remark on my appearance. I was trying to take in her first words.

'Who – *who* did you say?' I demanded.

'I said Sebastian, of course,' Fiona repeated. 'And by the way, I didn't know you knew him. Have you met him before in London or somewhere?'

'I don't know what on earth you're talking about,' I declared. 'I've never seen your silly Sebastian in my life.'

'Then why did you go swimming with him?' demanded Fiona, staring at my dripping hair.

'I didn't go swimming with him,' I exclaimed. 'I think you must have gone quite batty. I went swimming with the boy from the gardener's lodge.'

'But that *is* Sebastian, you idiot!'

I said nothing. My thoughts began to whirl. Frantically I tried to remember what I had said to Sebastian – if indeed it was he – and the more I thought, the more awful it became. When I remembered my last words, I grew cold with horror.

'You mean – you really mean that *that* was Sebastian?'

'If by "that" you mean the boy I saw you with out of the landing window just now, of course it was Sebastian. Who else could it be?'

'I – I thought he was the gardener's son,' I stammered. 'He told me distinctly he lived at the lodge at the bottom of the drive.'

'So he does,' put in Caroline, who had appeared by this time, and had somehow gathered what we were talking about. 'You see, as we said last night, Uncle Adrian, Sebastian's father, is frightfully poor, so we live here in the ancestral home and they live in the gardener's lodge. Sebastian says he likes it no end, and Uncle Adrian says it's a lot better to live there and keep it decent than to hang on here and let the old place go to rack and ruin.'

'Veronica thought Sebastian was the gardener's son!' Fiona said with a giggle. 'Gosh! Imagine Sebastian hoeing the cabbages! I must tell him that one!'

'Well, I shouldn't if I were you,' Caroline said quietly. 'If you do, it'll be a *faux* – whatever its name is – I mean the wrong thing to say, because Sebastian spent loads of time last hols weeding out the strawberry-bed. He's often told me that if he wasn't going to be a lawyer he'd very much like to be a gardener. He says it's a grand life watching things grow, and being out in the sun and wind all day long – loads better than working in a stuffy office in town.'

Fiona didn't know what to say to this so she turned her attention to my frock.

'Golly! I wonder what Sebastian thought of *that*?' she said, staring at it. 'It's like Joseph's coat of many colours in a thunderstorm!'

'I'll bet he wasn't rude enough to make personal remarks about it, anyway,' Caroline said pointedly.

Fiona grew red, but she couldn't think of anything more original to retort than: 'Mind your own business!'

53

'Do you two realize that the breakfast gong went ages ago,' Caroline went on calmly. 'Trixie's already called us twice. If you want any breakfast, you'd better stop discussing Sebastian and get a move on.'

'You were discussing him as much as anybody,' Fiona said sulkily.

I was so quiet at breakfast that Trixie got quite worried, and asked me whether the train had made me feel sick or if I was always as quiet as that. She also said that something would have to be done about my frock – I couldn't go about looking like that.

I glanced down at Mrs Crapper's bargain print sadly and in my heart I agreed with Fiona and Trixie – it *did* look rather as if it had been out in a thunderstorm, though it wasn't its fault, poor thing. After all, you can't expect an eightpence ha'penny-a-yard bargain print to be in 'fast' colours, can you?

'After breakfast we'll look out something for you to wear,' Trixie said from behind the teapot. 'Some shorts of Miss Fiona's, and a blouse, I think. You'd look nice in shorts, Miss Veronica, as you're so slim.'

Fiona didn't seem to approve of this remark.

'Veronica isn't any slimmer that I am,' she said indignantly. 'Anyway it isn't nice to be skinny, and I haven't any spare shorts.'

'You said last night you had,' Caroline said accusingly taking a large bite of toast. 'In fact, it was you who mentioned them.'

'Well, I made a mistake,' Fiona declared, spreading marmalade on a piece of bread and butter with great deliberation. 'I thought I had then, but now I find I haven't.'

'What about those khaki ones you said were too tight for you?' Caroline demanded. 'Only the other day you told Trixie—'

'Oh, shut up!' exclaimed Fiona. 'I wish you'd leave my clothes alone! If Veronica wants something to wear she can have my brown check frock.'

I was just about to observe that it wasn't *me* who wanted something to wear when Trixie settled the matter by getting really annoyed.

'I shall go through your clothes myself and decide what Miss Veronica is to wear, and that's flat,' she said with decision. 'Really, I never knew such children for arguments, and at breakfast-time too! . . .'

After breakfast Trixie was as good as her word, and I was presented with a pair of khaki shorts and a buttercup-yellow linen blouse to go with them. I brushed my dark hair till it shone, and then looked at myself in the long mirror of Fiona's wardrobe. I was no beauty, of course. My small face looked even thinner and paler than usual in contrast to Fiona's pink and white one. I was very slim – rude people might call me skinny, as Fiona had already done – and I wasn't even as tall as Caroline. My dark hair and eyes were my only consolation. All dancers like to have dark hair and eyes, though really I don't know why. Perhaps it's because it's the traditional style of a classical ballet dancer or perhaps it's because they show up well on the stage.

After Trixie had seen me and said I looked a great deal more like a young lady now, we went down to the kitchen to see Sheba, the Persian cat, who'd just had a family of gorgeous blue Persian kittens. While we were arguing about names for them, and had decided upon Cleopatra, Pharaoh and Tutankamen, Aunt June appeared at the kitchen door talking to Trixie about the lunch. She kissed us, and I thought she looked at me critically. As she went out, still talking to Trixie, I heard her say something that sounded like: 'What an amazing difference clothes make – the child looks almost pretty!'

My cheeks glowed. To anyone like Fiona who'd been considered beautiful all her life, a remark like this would have meant nothing. But to me, who'd always been thought a Plain Jane, it was like a bouquet.

'Almost pretty' – the words rang in my ears all the way to the kitchen garden, and lasted until we reached the gate that led out into the North Meadow where the ponies were grazing.

'Now for it!' Fiona exclaimed, propping open the gate with a handy log, which had obviously been used for the purpose many times. 'I only hope Melly won't be as hard to catch as she was yesterday. Thank goodness, Sebastian's already caught Warrior! He always makes her extra skittish.'

'Do you bring them into the stable every day?' I asked. 'I should have thought it would have been much nicer for them out here during the summer.'

Fiona stared at me coldly, and shrugged her shoulders, but Caroline attempted to explain:

'You see,' she said, 'they're hill ponies, so a lot of rich grass isn't good for them. They'd get far too fat for one thing, and they might even go lame. So in the spring and summer we bring them in here during the day. That's why we keep them in this field, too. The grass isn't nearly as rich as it is in the fields facing south. It's so near the moor, you see.'

'Oh, ' I said vaguely. 'I never thought of that.'

The field the ponies were in was certainly a great contrast to the lush meadows I'd caught glimpses of that morning when I'd made my sad attempt at running away. There the grass was long and rippling; here it was short, and there were patches of turf and marshy ground, where lovely moorland flowers were growing. There were several outcrops of rock too, with heather on them. The field was bounded on three sides by a rough drystone wall. I didn't know about drystone walls then, but Caroline explained to me later that all the walls in Northumberland used to be built without any plaster to hold the stones together, but, as the art is slowly dying out, more and more fences are being used. On the fourth side was a sombre little fir wood. Beyond the wall was open moorland, rising steeply in folds of purple and russet to a considerable height.

'That's Horsley Fell,' Caroline said, following my eyes. 'When you climb to the top you can see Three Tree Moor, and beyond that Corbie's Nob. There's a cairn on the top of the Nob to mark the highest point of the fell.'

We caught the ponies easily enough. At least we caught Caroline's Gilly – which was short for Gillyflower – and drove Fiona's Melisande through the gate and round into the stable yard. Finally we got her inside the building.

I tried not to get too friendly with the ponies, because it's no use hankering after something that isn't yours, and that you can never own. Still, I couldn't help gazing at Melisande's beautiful chestnut neck which Fiona was grooming till it shone like satin, and wishing that I was lucky enough to possess a pony all my own. Any sort of a pony would do for me; it wouldn't have to be an aristocratic chestnut like Melisande, or even a common or garden bay like Gillyflower. I felt that even a little broken-down pony would do for me. In some ways it would suit me better, because everyone knows that mongrel dogs have more affectionate natures than thoroughbreds and I expected it was the same with ponies. I was wrong, but I didn't know that then.

My thoughts were interrupted by a shout from Caroline.

'Here's Sebastian ... Coo-ee! We're here in the ponies' box!'

When I saw Sebastian's slim figure coming towards us, I felt awful. I shrank into the shadow of the stables, and wished that the floor would open and swallow me up. But of course it didn't, and I heard Sebastian say: 'Hullo, you two! Who's that hiding behind the corn bin?'

'It's Veronica,' Fiona said. 'You remember – she's our cousin. We told you about her.'

'Of course,' said Sebastian. Then he made me a mock bow. 'Methinks we have met before, lady!'

'We certainly have,' I said coldly. 'And I do think it was frightfully mean of you to take me in like that.'

'What? Oh, you mean the onions and things? Really, I felt it no end of a pity to curb your horticultural instincts!' said Sebastian with a grin. 'More than human nature could stand, in fact! You asked for it, you know, and when people ask me for anything I consider it discourteous not to give it to them. Besides, I was tickled to death at your character reading; it's not often a person hears exactly what another person thinks of them.'

'Well, you didn't hear what I thought of you,' I retorted, 'because I didn't know it *was* you. But you're hearing it now. I think you're perfectly beastly!'

'May you be forgiven!' said Sebastian devoutly, looking down his nose. 'You thought I was the perfect little gentleman – at the time, anyway. And if you didn't, you jolly well ought to have.' Then he changed the subject and said abruptly: 'You look jolly decent in those shorts, if you don't mind my saying so. In fact, I hardly recognized you ... shorts by Woolworth's – beg pardon, I mean Worth – without the Wool!'

'They're *my* shorts,' put in Fiona, sounding anything but pleased. 'I lent them to her.'

'No, you didn't,' Caroline said flatly. 'Trixie did. You said you hadn't any spare shorts. You wanted to lend her that mouldy old brown print frock that you knew she'd look ghastly in. *Anyone* would look the world's worst in that.'

'Pussy cat, pussy cat, where have you been?' sang Sebastian softly, openly enjoying the puzzled looks on both his cousins' faces, since neither of them knew which he meant. 'How about a ride,' he added, 'now that we've all been so painfully polite to each other?'

'We can't,' Fiona said with an angry glare at me, as though it were my fault that I was ponyless. '*She* hasn't got a mount.'

There was a short silence after this remark.

'Golly! I never thought of that,' Sebastian said at length. 'Suppose we go round to the farm and borrow old Mr What's-his-name's donkey. He goes OK, I've seen him. I'm pretty sure Mr What-do-you-call-him would let us have him for a bit.'

'You mean Septimus Keenliside of Pasture House?' queried Caroline.

Sebastian nodded.

'Yes – then we'd all have *something* to sit on, at any rate. We could teach Veronica to ride on our ponies, turn and turn about.'

'You aren't suggesting that I'm to ride Sep Keenliside's filthy little donkey, are you?' Fiona demanded.

Sebastian cocked an eyebrow in Fiona's direction.

'My good girl, I'm not suggesting anything. Far from it! You needn't join in the scheme if you don't want to. If you like to go riding your own pony all by yourself, I shouldn't dream of stopping you—'

'I should jolly well think not!' exploded Fiona. 'I'd like to see you try!'

'Bait me not, fair lady!' Sebastian said in mock heroic fashion. 'If you throw down the gauntlet, you'd look mighty queer if I picked it up! But as I was saying when you so rudely interrupted it's only if you come with *us* that you have to share. If you go off on your own, of course the question wouldn't arise. You couldn't share your pony then; there'd be no one to share it with, would there?'

Fiona looked as if she didn't quite know what to say to this statement, and before she had time to make up her mind,

Sebastian went on calmly: 'That's settled then – we ask Sep Keenliside for the loan of his donkey. All we want now is a saddle and bridle for the animal.'

'There are several snaffles that no one ever uses in the harness-room,' Caroline put in. 'And there's a saddle in the potting-shed. Goodness knows what it's doing there, but I saw it with my own eyes only yesterday.'

'I'll make a guess,' Sebastian drawled. 'It's there because Fiona dumped it down on the bench when she came in from a ride, and then forgot about it. Naughty! Naughty!'

'How dare you! I didn't!'

'Yes you did, Fiona. Sebastian's quite right, I remember now,' Caroline said. 'It was after the Pony Club meeting, ages ago – last autumn, in fact. It hasn't improved the look of it either, I can tell you! It's sprouting mould inches thick!'

'Well, let's go and salvage it!' Sebastian exclaimed. '"Ship ahoy!" "Scots wha hae wi Wallace bled", and all the usual oaths! We can clean it up.'

Suddenly Fiona leaped out of the hayloft where she'd been perched during the argument. She sprang in front of us and stood right in the doorway.

'That's *my* saddle!' she yelled. 'Veronica can't have my saddle!'

'*Your* saddle?' queried Sebastian, with raised eyebrows. 'If it's the one you had at the Pony Club, I have a vague idea it was in the harness-room long before your people took over Bracken Hall, my child. So by rights it belongs to my father.'

'*We're* living in the house now,' flashed Fiona, 'so everything that's in it is ours.'

'Oh, ho! So that's what you think, is it?' Sebastian retorted. 'Chummy view of life, what! Let's not pursue the argument any further, it offendeth my sense of – of – well, in short, it isn't – you know what I mean.'

'I *don't* know what you mean, you horrible boy, and I don't believe you do yourself, either,' Fiona yelled, aware that Sebastian was laughing at her.

'Granted,' Sebastian said calmly. 'Blame it on to my Irish grandmother.'

I stared at him thoughtfully. He was quite a different person from the serious boy I had talked to in the train about ballet, and argued with about running away in the early morning. I suspected – and later knew quite definitely – that not many people saw the serious side of Sebastian. In fact, only a handful of his closest friends knew that it was there at all.

'*Have* you got an Irish grandmother?' I asked curiously.

Sebastian nodded.

'Yes, rather! Old girl pegged out twenty years ago. She's in Heaven now – if she isn't in the other place! I rather suspect the latter. Everyone says I take after her. I hope so! Jolly old girl – if you can go by the family records. Used to traipse about dear old Ireland in one of those jaunting-cars. Turned up at all the race meetings – even when she was eighty – and woe betide anyone who impeded her line of vision! She landed him one with her umbrella!'

'I believe you're making all that up,' Caroline said accusingly. 'Everything I've heard about old Granny O'Rourke was perfectly respectable, and anyway she lived in Devonshire.'

'She retired there when she was old,' Sebastian said, not a bit taken aback. 'On her ninety-fifth birthday. I remember it as if it were yesterday.'

Then seeing Caroline's mouth open to make a crushing reply to this statement, he added quickly: 'Well, let's get back to the point, shall we? We were talking about a saddle, if you remember. You hardly ever use it Fiona; in fact you've never used it since the day we mentioned, and that's eight months ago. You'd never even have thought about it if I hadn't said we'd lend it to Veronica.'

'You're *not* going to lend it to Veronica!'

61

'Oh, yes I am, you selfish little beast!'

'You're not! I forbid it! Just because Veronica's new, you try to curry favour—'

Fiona stopped with a gasp. Sebastian's blue eyes had narrowed, and his face had gone quite white with fury.

'Be quiet! You say another word and you'll be sorry for it!'

Fiona didn't say another word. I think that for once in her life she was scared.

'Get out of my way!' ordered Sebastian in a furious voice. Then he got hold of himself and dropped back into his usual bantering tone: 'Roll up! Roll up, ladies and gents! World-famous wrestling champion, Bumpemoffski, about to perform one of his prodigious feats of strength! Watch him throw lady over his left shoulder clean into horse's manger ...' he advanced upon Fiona purposefully.

But Fiona didn't wait for any more. She turned and fled away up the garden path, dashed into the little potting-shed that stood by the wicket-gate leading into the kitchen garden, and banged the door behind her.

'Open this door!' yelled Sebastian when we reached the place a moment or two later.

There was no answer.

'She's bolted it,' Caroline said, as we rattled the sneck.

'Open the door!' Sebastian ordered in a tone of voice that showed quite plainly he hadn't yet got over the insult that Fiona had flung at him before she'd fled. 'If you don't open it, I shall break it in.'

Still there was silence.

'Right-ho! Then here goes!' he put his shoulder to the door, the rusty bolt gave way and the door flew wide.

We all crowded in. Fiona was standing underneath the tiny window with a queer expression on her face – triumphant I think I'd call it – and there was a strong smell of disinfectant that stifled even the smell of mould, damp and dust. The saddle lay, as Caroline had said, on the little bench that stretched along one side of the shed. Sebastian picked it up; then dropped it again very quickly,

'What's up? Is it as bad as all that?' Caroline said anxiously, as Sebastian rubbed his hands on a heap of dry leaves.

'Oh, golly! it's all – all – what on earth is it?'

'Creosote,' Sebastian said shortly. 'The little tick's emptied the whole tin over it!'

It was only too true! The saddle was mouldy no longer. It was a disgusting wet mess of creosote; impossible for anyone to touch, much less ride upon. A large empty creosote tin stood in the corner – silent witness of Fiona's crime.

Sebastian's mouth curled.

'Crude!' he drawled. 'Very crude, my dear cousin! Well, now as you haven't got a saddle—'

'You mean Veronica hasn't got one,' Fiona corrected sweetly.

'As I was saying,' Sebastian continued, 'when you so rudely interrupted, Veronica will have to use *your* saddle now. So, as you haven't got another one for yourself, there's not much point in you coming with us, is there?' He waved us out of the shed, shut the door again, and lashed it firmly with an end of rope that was lying near, seemingly oblivious to Fiona's scream of fury from within.

'How dare you! I'll get out somehow!' she yelled.

'Well, I advise you not to try the window,' drawled Sebastian. 'If you do, you'll be in a jam – literally! And by the way,' he added softly through a crack in the door, 'you'd better not try any more fancy work on that saddle. If you do, I'll go one better with yours – with white paint! It'll look like a blinking wedding cake when I've done with it!'

He retreated from the hut and its furious occupant singing cheerfully:

'Here comes the bride,
Fifty inches wide! . . .'

We all yelled together:

'Here comes the groom,
Although there's hardly room!'

Chapter 6

Bacon and Shakespeare

I don't know whether you've had any experience of donkeys. If you haven't, then you're lucky! If you have, you'll know what was in store for us when we trooped into Sep Keenliside's field, having first asked his permission, of course. We had also got permission to borrow his donkey – if we could catch him.

'Of course we'll catch him,' I said rather scornfully, I'm afraid. In those days I didn't know much about animals; I'm wiser now! 'A donkey isn't like a racehorse. He may be a bit slow and obstinate, but he won't be hard to catch—'

'U – um,' Sebastian said doubtfully, being country bred.

We began our task. Round and round that field we walked and Sep Keenliside's donkey walked round in front of us. It was like a procession! Then we tried running, and the donkey trotted. We trotted. We tried heading him off, but he dodged us; we tried cornering him, but go near a corner he wouldn't. Finally the others said that they'd go and get the ponies, and see if they were more successful when mounted.

'All right,' I panted. 'I'll wait for you here.' I sank down on the grass at the edge of the field, exhausted.

It wasn't long before they were back again, Caroline riding Gilly, and Sebastian his chestnut gelding, Warrior.

'By the way, Fiona's got out of that place,' Caroline told me. 'She must have yelled and someone's let her out.'

'She was lucky!' said Sebastian. 'Not many people go into there as a general rule. Well, if she goes riding, she'll have to

65

do it bareback because we've got the one and only saddle' – he motioned to Fiona's saddle that lay beside me on the grass, waiting until we had caught the donkey. 'Anyone got any bright ideas about nabbing him?'

'Perhaps if we walk up to him softly and call him by his name he might let us catch him,' I said. 'By the way, what *is* his name?'

'It's Shakespeare,' Sebastian told me. Then, seeing my astonished face, he added: 'You see, there's usually a pig in this field, and that pig is a bosom pal of old Shakespeare's; so we call 'em Bacon and Shakespeare! Get the idea?'

'Sort of,' I said jumping up. 'Well anyway, let's try it.'

The others dismounted, tethered their ponies to the railings and the operation began.

But Shakespeare didn't respond to the coaxing any more than he had to the chasing. Sometimes he let us get within a few yards of his tail, but never near enough to grab him.

After this we tried with the ponies but this was even worse. The animals seemed to excite Shakespeare and he grew terribly frisky, galloping about like mad and kicking up his heels. I began to feel quite nervous! It wasn't that I was afraid of falling off, but I was terribly scared I'd break or sprain something, for this would mean the end of my dancing career.

'I – I'm wondering—' I said to Sebastian, as we retired for a breather underneath the one tree the field possessed, 'I'm wondering whether after all I *ought* to ride, because of – well, you know what I told you yesterday?'

'Oh, the dancing!' Sebastian said seriously, his eyes on Caroline, who was still trying vainly to trap Shakespeare in a far corner of the field. 'Well, I shouldn't let it stop you riding, if I were you – not at this stage, anyway. It's not as if you were a *prima ballerina*, and I should think it would improve you – slim your thighs and calves, and make you nice and strong, being out in the fresh air, I mean.'

'But supposing I fell off?' I said anxiously. 'It's not that I'm *afraid*, you know, but—'

'Of course I know that,' said Sebastian. 'You wouldn't have far to fall, though – not on old Sep Keenliside's donkey, would you? He's only about nine hands—'

'Nine hands?' I echoed.

'Oh, don't you know – that's the way you measure horses. A hand is four inches. So you see he's not very big.'

'No, I suppose not,' I admitted with a smile. 'I expect you're right.'

By this time Caroline had returned crestfallen, and we all decided to call it a day – for the time being, at any rate.

'We'll come back after lunch with a rope, and lasso the little blighter, if all else fails!' declared Sebastian with determination. 'Can't be beaten by a donkey!'

We took Fiona's saddle into the house with us, and Sebastian sat on it all through lunch, much to Trixie's disgust. Fortunately, though, the meal was in the schoolroom, so there were no other grown-ups there, and Sebastian, I had already found, could twist Trixie round his little finger when he wanted to. She grumbled and said she didn't know what modern children were coming to, that in her young days people sat on Christian chairs, and not on nasty heathen saddles, but that she supposed if Sebastian couldn't eat his dinner in any other way, she'd have to put up with the contraption, but it wasn't her idea of how a young gentleman ought to behave at table.

Sebastian solemnly assured her that he couldn't possibly eat as much as a spoonful of blancmange, sitting on a chair: 'And anyway,' he added, giving me a sidelong look, 'I'm not a young gentleman, am I, Veronica?'

'Whatever do you mean, Master Sebastian?' demanded Trixie indignantly.

67

'Veronica knows!' Sebastian said, winking at me behind Trixie's back.

After the meal was over we returned to the attack. Fiona hadn't come with us; she'd gone off on Melisande without a saddle, and I must say it was peaceful without her.

'If we could only get the little beggar through the gate into the lane,' Sebastian said as we reached Sep Keenliside's field once more, 'he'd be in a trap. We could nab him easily in that narrow space.'

But alas! Shakespeare saw the trap as well or better than we did. He just wouldn't go through that gate. Every time we got him up to it, he swerved, and was away over the field with a kick of his heels, leaving us standing looking silly.

Suddenly Sebastian gave a shout.

'Gosh! I've got it! ...' He dashed away before Caroline and I'd had time to ask what it was he'd got, and disappeared into the lane. Presently there came the sound of grunts and squeals from the other side of the gate.

For a moment we were completely taken in.

'It's the farm pig we told you about – the one Shakespeare loves like a brother!' yelled Caroline. 'It's jolly old Bacon! No, it's not; it's *Sebastian*!'

Somebody else was taken in as well as we were, and that was Shakespeare. His ears waggled, he gave a delighted bray, then trotted off through the gate as meek as a mouse!

'Got him!' yelled Sebastian, jumping up and slamming the gate shut. 'What a blessing I'm so good at imitating animals.'

We couldn't say anything to this modest remark, because for the moment we'd been taken in ourselves, and there was no denying the fact that he *was* good.

We found it very easy to catch Shakespeare after this. In fact, when he found himself cornered, he gave himself up. We saddled and bridled him, and then began the business of teaching me to ride him.

'It's terribly queer teaching anyone to ride a donkey,' Sebastian said in a rather worried manner when I had at last succeeded in scrambling upon Shakespeare's back. 'You've just *got* to tell them to do all the wrong things, such as kicking him like mad, or walloping him, because he won't go at all if you don't.'

It was only too true. In fact even walloping wouldn't make Shakespeare move much faster than a snail, which was queer because in the field he'd charged around as if he were winning the Derby! The only way to make him trot was for someone to ride behind and keep sloshing him on the hindquarters with a riding-crop. And even this had its drawbacks, because Shakespeare resented the sloshing and showed it by buck-jumping, and turfing me off into the nearest clump of nettles. Not dangerous, but most undignified and distinctly painful!

After a bit, Sebastian suggested that it was time we began our turn-and-turn-about scheme, and said he'd take on Shakespeare.

Anyway,' he added, 'I think Veronica had better learn to ride on one of our ponies. It takes a really experienced horseman to manage a donkey! Perhaps you'd better let her have Gilly, Caroline, and ride Warrior yourself. Might be safer!'

I must say I was thankful I hadn't to mount Warrior. For one thing I felt I was nearer the ground on Gillyflower, and for another she didn't dance and show the whites of her eyes quite as much as Sebastian's pony did.

Well, by four o'clock we'd had a good afternoon's sport though, as Sebastian had said before, you could hardly call it a riding lesson.

'In fact, though I hate to admit it, I feel that Sep Keenliside's donkey isn't such a very good idea after all,' he confessed. 'We'll have to think of something else.' We reined in our mounts and stood still where we were, thinking deeply, Caroline and I on the ponies and Sebastian, his legs trailing in the grass, astride the Immortal Bard – by that I mean old Shakespeare. Incidentally, Shakespeare passed the time away by scratching his tummy with his hind leg and yawning.

Suddenly Caroline gave a yell:

'*I've* got it!'

'Fetch a butterfly-net quick somebody,' drawled Sebastian. 'Caroline's got it – rare, almost unknown specimen. Looks to me very much like a daddy-long-legs . . .'

'Do shut up!' Caroline said, cutting him short. 'I wish you'd try to be serious for just two seconds. How about *hiring* a mount for Veronica?'

'Hiring?' echoed Sebastian. 'Excellent scheme. Only snag as far as I can see is the financial question. Cash – or rather the lack of it.'

'Cash?' echoed Caroline in her turn, as if she'd never heard of it.

'Cash I said, and cash I meant,' went on Sebastian. 'In other words tin, brass, filthy lucre. Call it what you will. Personally I haven't a bean.'

'Neither have I,' I said, feeling a trifle guilty. 'Not enough to hire a pony, that is.' I must explain here that the guilty feeling was due to the fact that I wasn't absolutely penniless. I did possess a small amount of money of my own – a pound or two – but it was earmarked for more important things than hiring ponies; things that I didn't think Caroline, at any rate, would understand: such as ballet shoes, perhaps even ballet lessons. I was quite determined to keep the small amount of capital I had intact for the golden opportunity if ever it came.

'I suppose Caroline's got oodles of the stuff,' Sebastian went on. 'Else she wouldn't have trotted out her brainwave?'

Caroline grew red.

'No, as a matter of fact, I haven't a bean either,' she confessed. 'We'll have to make money somehow. How *do* people make money, Sebastian?'

'Well, the quickest way would be to burgle the bank,' Sebastian suggested helpfully. 'Or a rather safer way, though less exciting, would be to embezzle the fortune of some rich old aunt who trusts you with he last shilling. Or then again, one might break the bank at Monte Carlo.'

'You are beastly,' Caroline said. 'I do wish you'd come out with something sensible.'

'Well, how about a Bring and Buy Sale?' I put in. 'When we wanted funds for anything in our parish we always had a Bring and Buy.'

'Jolly good idea,' Caroline declared. 'But what happens if people just *don't* – bring and buy, I mean. Or if they don't turn up at all? I have an idea they wouldn't if we asked them. You see, we aren't like the Women's Institute—'

'I should just think not!' Sebastian said in such a horrified voice that we couldn't help laughing. 'There's nothing I should hate more than being like the Women's Institute.'

'I didn't mean that at all, idiot!' exclaimed Caroline. 'I meant – goodness, what *did* I mean?'

'Take it as said,' drawled Sebastian. 'Only don't ask me, that's all. I felt it was a trifle mixed at the time. Well, let's wash out the Bring and Buy, and make it a Wayside Stall like the cricket club had last summer. We could nab all the cars coming past—'

'Or we could have it in the village hall,' Caroline said.

Sebastian shrugged his shoulders.

'Now I ask you – how could a Wayside Stall be in the village hall? Sounds like a popular song!'

'The cricket club had one there last Whit-Monday,' declared Caroline triumphantly. 'So what?'

For once Sebastian was silent.

'OK,' he said at length. 'Have it your own way. We'll have a Wayside Stall in the village hall.'

'As a matter of fact I think it *would* be better here, outside the gates,' admitted Caroline rather sheepishly. 'I like your idea of nabbing the cars; besides we'd be able to crash into your house, Sebastian, and make lemonade for the people in the cars. Twopence a glass!'

'Well, I'm dashed!' exclaimed Sebastian. 'After all that arguing! How like a girl!'

'What sort of things would we sell?' I broke in, seeing that Caroline was beginning to get really annoyed. 'At home we used to collect up "white elephants" – things people didn't want.'

'I know!' yelled Caroline. 'There's Mummy's tea-service – the one in the cabinet in the drawing-room.'

'Oh, but we couldn't go selling tea-services,' I objected. 'Most especially not Aunt June's.'

'I wasn't exactly thinking of selling it,' explained Caroline. 'I thought we'd put it on the stall marked SOLD, like they do at the Women's Institute garden fêtes when anyone wants anything special. It would make the stall *look* good.'

'Sounds a batty idea,' Sebastian declared, 'but if it's the done thing at these shows, it's OK with me. We mustn't scandalize Veronica, though. I'm sure they didn't do such lawless things in London.'

I laughed.

'We did worse than that!' Then I was silent. It had suddenly occurred to me that I had never once thought of London since before breakfast!

Chapter 7

The Wayside Stall

We chose Saturday for our Wayside Stall as we thought more cars were likely to pass on that day than on any other except Sunday, and of course we couldn't have a Wayside Stall on a Sunday – the whole village would be scandalized. Fortunately, Aunt June was away that afternoon, and Trixie had gone into Newcastle to see about school clothes for Fiona and Caroline, so we were left with a clear field. I found that Sebastian had been right about Bracken Hall and that, apart from meals, we didn't spend much of our time indoors. In fact, the grownups seemed quite glad to get rid of us, and as long as Sebastian was with us nobody seemed to mind where we went or what we did.

I wish you could have seen the things we collected for our stall. Sebastian went round the village with a handcart – borrowed from the Boy Scouts who used it to collect jumble in – and came back with a dozen tennis balls that the moths had got at and didn't bounce, an ancient kitchen fender that had once been someone's pride and joy but had since been parked in an outhouse and had turned green; a pair of Wellington boots that leaked; two ladies' handbags with broken catches; and a doll with no legs.

Caroline and I went round the big houses in the district and our haul was a stuffed owl in a case; a silver-plated soup tureen with all the silver plate worn off; a tin bath with a hole in the bottom; three pairs of Venetian blinds; and a bathchair. Fiona refused to collect anything; she said she drew the line at begging, but that she'd help with the refreshments if we liked.

'OK. But if you do, you'll have to wash up the glasses, as well, I warn you,' Sebastian said.

'Oh, all right,' Fiona said rather sulkily. I think she thought the whole affair somewhat beneath her dignity, but she didn't want to be left out of it, all the same.

We set out our stall on the wide grass verge near the lodge gates, and waited for our customers, Aunt June's tea-service having the place of honour in the middle. But alas! There were shoals of cars with masses of people in them passing all the time, but not one of them stopped. After a bit, we got desperate, and Sebastian wrote a large notice which said:

DANGER!
YOU DON'T KNOW WHAT YOU ARE
MISSING!

But even this didn't do the trick. I think some of the people actually thought it was a joke; anyway they grinned at us and waved as they shot past. Terribly aggravating!

When quite an hour had gone by, we changed our tactics. Caroline stood bang in the middle of the road brandishing the tureen lid in one hand and the legless doll in the other just as an especially big and palatial-looking car came rushing round the corner.

'Hey! Wouldn't you like to buy something at our Wayside Stall?' she yelled.

The car swung to a standstill with a jerk – it jolly well had to, or commit a murder! – and the occupants swept supercilious eyes over our collection of white elephants.

'How quaint!' said one of them, getting out of the car and poking one of the Wellington boots. 'You haven't any home-made cakes, or fruit, little girl, have you? No fresh eggs, or poultry? . . .'

'Our stall is a white elephant stall,' Sebastian said firmly. 'Cakes and fruit aren't what you might call white elephants; neither is poultry.'

'No, they aren't, are they?' tinkled the lady with an odious smile at her companion who was still sitting in the car. Incidentally Sebastian called that smile a leer when we talked the matter over afterwards. 'Have you got any refreshments?'

'Oh yes – we've got lemonade. Fizzy-Fountain,' Caroline said eagerly. 'Twopence a glass.'

'It's not terribly nice,' put in Fiona. 'I didn't want them to have it, but they would. The bottle's been in the schoolroom cupboard for simply ages and it's frightfully flat – even with the bicarbonate of soda that Sebastian put in to make it fizz.'

We glared at Fiona, while the supercilious lady exchanged another meaning glance with her companion.

'You can give me a glass,' she said at length. 'John! Would you like a glass of Fizzy-Fountain lemonade, with a dash of bicarbonate in to freshen it up? These quaint children are selling it for something or other.'

'Good Lord, no!' said John. 'I can think of nothing I should hate more! ... Fizzy-Fountain lemonade! ... Bicarbonate of soda! ... Good Lord!'

He hastily ran up the car window as if we were going to produce a hose with lemonade and drown him with it – which I must say I'd have dearly loved to do.

'I feel much the same way myself,' said the lady, 'but one feels one must humour children. Thank you, dear' – this to Caroline who had appeared with the glass. Then, to our horror, she took the glass, poured the contents into the hedge, and laid down twopence on our stall. After which she got back into the car and the two of them drove away.

'Well ...' we said. 'If only she'd let one of *us* drink it, it wouldn't have been so bad. But a whole glass of that gorgeous stuff wasted.' We gazed sadly at the patch of damp grass that lay flattened, silent witness of the wasteful sin that had been committed by the car-owning lady.

'Or if she'd only drunk it herself,' Sebastian said, 'it wouldn't have made us feel so cheap. After all,' he added gloomily, 'it wouldn't have poisoned her.'

'It *might*!' put in Fiona with a superior smile.

'What on earth did you go saying that for about bicarbonate of soda?' exploded Caroline. 'You know very well that the stuff wasn't flat – we only put the bicarbonate in to make it fizz still more. If you hadn't given the show away she'd just have thought how nice it was.'

'It was only fair to warn her,' Fiona insisted.

Sebastian stared at his cousin thoughtfully for a few seconds.

'I've wondered more than once why you wanted to be in this show at all, Fiona,' he said. 'But if you have ideas of sabotaging it, you can give them up here and now, or get out.'

Fiona stared back at him; then she laughed and said scornfully: 'Well, I hope trade keeps good, and that you don't all collapse with exhaustion in the rush-hour!' After which she turned her back on us and walked away towards the house.

We sat down with our backs to the Wayside Stall, lost in our gloomy thoughts. Half the afternoon gone, and all we had made was twopence.

By teatime we were desperate. Half the village seemed to have heard of our stall and had trekked along to inspect it. But although we had begged them to think of the usefulness of a tin bath, even if it *had* a hole in the bottom, and Sebastian had offered the bathchair practically with tears in his eyes, they hadn't bought a thing – not even a glass of lemonade. Lots of the village kids came along too and jeered at us. They stood in a crowd on the opposite side of the road and said rude things about our white elephants. Two prominent members of the Women's Institute pounced on Aunt June's tea-service and

76

wanted to know how much it was, but when we explained firmly that it was sold, and pointed to the notice propped up against one of the dark blue and gold cups, they just looked at each other significantly in that maddening way grown-ups have, and went away muttering that they were sure our parents didn't know what was going on and that somebody ought to tell them.

'Old cats!' Caroline said to their retreating backs. 'Fiona always said Mrs Musgrave was a cat.'

'Fiona was right for once,' Sebastian declared, and began to sing:

> 'Pussy cat, pussy cat, what do you mean
> By being so terribly awfully mean? . . .

'You can't say that,' I broke in. 'It doesn't rhyme. I mean, it's two words the same.'

'I don't consider Mrs Musgrave deserves a rhyme that rhymes,' declared Sebastian. 'Anyway, the next bit's smashing! It goes:

> 'You could at least have bought a tureen
> To set before the king, not to mention the queen.'

'It doesn't scan,' I objected.

'You're too pernickety,' pronounced Sebastian. 'Look out! Here's another car. Golly, it's actually stopping!'

A gentleman and a lady got out. The man had a little black beard and wore a black, large-brimmed hat made of something that looked like velvet, and his coat was made of velvet too. His trousers were blue, and wide, and flapped as he walked, and his flowing tie and socks were orange, with little scarlet fishes on them. The lady wore wine-coloured corduroy slacks, flat-heeled shoes of red stuff like cork, and huge blue sunglasses. We blinked as we looked at the two of them.

'Oh, Claude!' exclaimed the lady, picking up a cup and turning it this way and that, so that the gold on it caught the light. 'Surely a real Crown Derby tea-service!'

Hastily we explained for the umpteenth time that afternoon that Aunt June's tea-set wasn't for sale. Really, it's amazing how many grown-up people don't seem able to read!

'Oh...' said the lady in a very disappointed-sounding voice. 'I thought it was too good to be true.'

'We've some Fizzy-F ...' I was beginning, when the man gave an excited sort of yelp.

'Look here, Yvonne. This is interesting ...' He had picked up one of the paintings that I'd done in Jonathan's studio. Trixie had found them in the bottom of my trunk, and I'd only just been in time to stop her burning them. We'd had the happy idea of putting them on the stall. Not that we thought anyone would buy them but, as Sebastian said, they would brighten it up a bit. One was a still-life – tomatoes, a cucumber, and a lustre bowl that Jonathan loved as a brother; the other consisted of a red Paisley shawl draped over a pale duck-egg blue figure made of something that looked like soap.

'Who painted these?' demanded the man, looking at us in turn.

'I did,' I answered. Then I saw that he had turned the canvases over and was looking at the proper sides. 'Oh – *those*? Jonathan did those,' I added.

'Jonathan who, dear?' said the lady with the glasses.

'Jonathan Rosenbaum. He lived on the floor higher up than us in London.'

'You mean *the* Jonathan Rosenbaum?' persisted the lady.

'All I know is that Jonathan painted those pictures and that his name is Rosenbaum. He said those canvases made him feel sick, and that I was doing him a favour when I daubed on the back side of them.'

'Well – can you beat that, Claude?' said the lady. 'To find a Rosenbaum on a village Wayside Stall! Can you beat it?'

'No,' said the bearded man. 'But there you are – life is full of surprises!' Then he turned to us again: 'Look here, kids. Are these things your own? I mean, can you sell them?'

'Of *course* we can sell them!' I exclaimed, stopping myself just in time from adding: 'What do you think a Wayside Stall is for?' Really, grown-up people are exasperating sometimes!

'Well, I'll give you a guinea apiece for them,' went on the bearded gentleman, clasping the canvases to his breast as if he feared we might snatch them away again. 'Is that enough?'

'A – guinea – apiece?' we gasped, almost too astonished to answer. 'Golly!' Then Sebastian managed to stammer: 'I should just say it is enough! A guinea apiece – golly! Thank you most awfully, sir.'

'Thank *you*,' said the man with the beard, and he laid two one-pound notes on the Wayside Stall, and dropped two shillings into the soup tureen with a tinkle. Come along, Yvonne.' Then he made us a little bow and said again even more fervently: 'Thank *you*.'

'You'd really think we'd done him a favour,' Sebastian said thoughtfully, looking after the pair as they hopped back into the tourer and drove away. 'By the way, Veronica, who *is* your Mr Rosenbaum? They seemed to think an awful lot of him.'

'I haven't the least idea who Jonathan is,' I answered. 'At least I don't know who his father was, or what public school he went to, if that's what you mean. I shouldn't think Jonathan ever went to school at all. He's – well, somehow I can't imagine Jonathan going to school. He just wouldn't fit in.'

'But what sort of an artist is he?' persisted Sebastian. 'Has he had any pictures in the Royal Academy, for instance?'

'The Royal Academy?' I repeated. 'Oh, yes – I think so. But Jonathan doesn't think much of the Royal Academy. He says the Royal Academy is the dullest, stuffiest institution ever set up by a group of stuffy Englishmen – and that's saying something! He's exhibited there, but he despises it, really.'

'Um – he sounds a queer sort of cove!' said Sebastian. 'Does he ever sell any of his pictures?'

'Oh, yes – a few,' I answered. 'He's very well known, really. But of course he doesn't make an awful lot of money – Jonathan says no real artists do – not until they're dead. He says only fashionable portrait painters make money, and they only do it by imperilling their immortal souls and flattering a lot of horse-faced society women.'

'Well, those people in the car evidently knew him,' Caroline put in. 'And we've actually made some money. Two whole guineas! Three cheers for Jonathan, I say, however queer he may be! Golly! If it hadn't been for Veronica's pictures, we'd have made exactly twopence – not much use for hiring a pony. Awful thought, isn't it?'

'Tell you what,' said Sebastian. 'Let's go into the cottage and scoff all that gorgeous Fizzy-Fountain stuff. It's clear that nobody wants it.'

'Yes – *let's*!' we said in chorus.

Chapter 8

Arabesque

You've no idea what a difficult job it is hiring a pony. It's not that there aren't any animals available, but none of them seemed exactly what we needed – according to Sebastian, anyway. Sebastian took the matter into his own hands, and guaranteed to find me the ideal mount. But after we had looked at what seemed to be hundreds of ponies of all colours, ages, and sizes, I began to feel that it wasn't as easy as it had seemed when we began.

Not so Sebastian. He was still quite cheerful. Moreover he still appeared to be perfectly confident that, provided we looked long and far enough, we'd find what we were looking for sooner or later.

'Now let's see,' he said, consulting his notebook, and biting the end of his pencil thoughtfully, 'after discarding all the absolutely hopeless ones, like that half-broken gelding that behaved like a bucking-bronco-in-a-fit every time you got on his back, we're left with the following:

'(1) Mr Drummond of Ditchfield – black mare, ten years, twelve hands. An awful slug – nearly as bad as Keenliside's donkey. Shouldn't wonder if she isn't broken-winded into the bargain!

'(2) Mrs Lawes of Sandibraes – chestnut filly, rising four, eleven three. Too young, and a bit small. Anyway, a bit skittish for Veronica to begin on.

'(3) Sandy Mcfarlane, Four-Lane-Ends – bay filly, twelve

hands. Much too stocky. Back like the kitchen table. Give you bow legs, Veronica!'

'Oh,' I wouldn't have him – I mean her – not for anything!' I said in such a horrified voice that they all laughed. 'What others are there?'

'Only that piebald mare from the riding school,' answered Sebastian with a sigh.

'What was wrong with her?' I demanded. 'She seemed an awfully nice pony to me.'

'So she was – as long as you didn't leave the neighbourhood of the riding school,' said Sebastian with a laugh. 'But you try to ride her over in this direction. Nappy isn't the word, I can tell you! Of course we *might* cure her in time, but after all, we're *hiring* the animal, not buying it. We don't want to spend all our time curing its faults for someone else to benefit. Anyway, I don't think a nappy pony is much good for a beginner.'

'Well, if there aren't any more, what do we do?' I asked.

'Think deeply,' replied Sebastian. 'We've still got that man who lives at the inn by the bridge at Merlingford. Someone said he had a nice little pony they were sure he would let out on hire. If it turns out to be a dud, we'll just *have* to fall back on one of these. I think it's a toss-up between the riding-school one and Mr Drummond's mare. We might brighten the latter up a bit with a spot of corn. But we'll investigate the Merlingford pony first. "Never cross your bridges before you come to them" is my motto!'

'Except the Merlingford bridge!' laughed Caroline.

Our luck was in. According to Sebastian the Merlingford pony was the very thing. Keen, but not too frisky for me to learn on. Just the right size – twelve hands. His age didn't really matter, because, as Sebastian said, we weren't buying him. But as a matter of fact he was eight. He was what I called grey, but

Sebastian called him a blue-roan, and he wasn't too stocky.

'I think there's no fear of your becoming bow-legged,' Sebastian assured me.

I looked at him suspiciously.

'I believe you're making fun of me.'

'On such a grave matter as legs straying from the vertical I would not dare to joke,' Sebastian said in mock solemnity. Then he turned in his toes and walked off down the road, swaying from side to side and looking so exactly like a racing jockey that we all burst out laughing.

'He is an idiot!' giggled Caroline.

'It's no use – Sebastian can't be serious for one minute,' Fiona put in. 'Really, I don't know how Uncle Adrian stands him!'

'You stand him yourself very well,' Caroline declared. 'You only came this afternoon because Sebastian was here. You know very well you're not a bit interested in Veronica's pony, really.'

'You shut up!' ordered Fiona, turning red.

When Sebastian came back, we asked the man at the inn – his name was Tompkinson – how much he wanted for the hire of his pony. To our horror he said ten bob the day.

'Oh, but we don't want him for just one day,' Sebastian explained. 'We want him for several months – two anyway. Perhaps we may want him for a very long time, if we can get up another Wayside Stall to pay for him. Honestly, it'd be worth your while to let us have him cheap. We'd give you cash down,' he added hastily, as the man looked at us doubtfully, and he took the two one-pound notes out of his breeches' pocket and rustled them.

Mr Tompkinson scratched his head and said all right – 'seven and six the day.'

'Nothing doing,' said Sebastian. 'Still far too much.' Then he walked round the pony – we were back in the stable yard by this time – and looked at it critically. 'He's not a terribly keen animal, is he?' he added. 'Wouldn't suit anybody but a beginner. He would do for Veronica to learn on, though. We'll give you three and six a week.'

'Split the difference and make it five bob,' said Mr Tompkinson cheerfully, which seemed to me queer since he was losing such a lot of money on the deal.

'Right-ho,' answered Sebastian equally cheerfully. 'Five bob it is.' He laid down the two one-pound notes on the edge of the horse-trough. 'That'll do for eight weeks. Would you mind giving me a receipt.'

Mr Tompkinson scribbled on a bit of paper, torn off the back of an old envelope, words to the effect that we had paid for the hire of his pony, Prince, for eight weeks, signed it, and the deed was done.

'Prince?' echoed Caroline as we left the stable yard, Sebastian leading the pony by the bridle, which was included in the terms of the hiring, as also the saddle – we had made that clear. 'Golly! What a name! Let's change it.'

'Unlucky to change a horse's name,' pronounced Sebastian.

'A lot you care about superstition!' retorted Caroline. 'Let's call him something romantic like Nomad, or Petulengro, after the gipsy.'

'Petulengro?' Sebastian said with a grimace. 'Too long! Can't be shortened, either. Fancy yelling out: "Petty. Petty! Come here, will you!" Anyway, he's Veronica's pony. How about Veronica choosing his name?'

'Yes, of course,' Caroline said at once. 'Those were only suggestions. Go on, Veronica.'

Fiona looked scornful, but she didn't say anything. I couldn't help feeling glad it happened to be my pictures, or rather Jonathan's, that had made the money to hire the pony.

'I'll call him Arab – short for Arabesque,' I said after a moment's thought.

'Jolly good name,' Sebastian declared.

'I think it's awful,' declared Fiona. 'He's not an Arab. He's not even black. And what's an *arabesque*, anyway?'

'It's a position in dancing, ignoramus,' Sebastian told her. 'Something Veronica has learned to do that you'll never learn – not until you stop pinching the cream off the top of the trifle. You're too fat!'

'You beast! I'm not too fat. I'm not fat at all!' Fiona yelled.

As a matter of fact she wasn't, and Sebastian was only teasing, but Fiona really hadn't got much sense of humour and she was usually taken in by him. After her outburst she rode on ahead of us and sulked, while Sebastian gave me a riding lesson. He showed me how to mount, telling me not to dig my pony in the ribs while I was doing it, if I didn't want him to charge off without me. To spring up into the saddle, instead of hauling myself there by the reins.

'You must be a spring balance not a haulage contractor if you want to learn to ride properly,' he said as I mounted for the umpteenth time. 'There – I think you've got the idea now. You'd better stay up.' He patted Arab's neck reassuringly. 'He's a dashed good little pony.'

I looked at Sebastian in astonishment.

'You didn't say that to poor Mr Tompkinson.'

Sebastian grinned sheepishly.

'Oh, I forgot about that little bit of by-play! Well, I had to say *something* to make the fellow bring his price down, hadn't I? Anyway, he didn't believe me. It's all part of the game. When the horse trots in at the stable door, truth flies out at the window, as the saying goes! By horse I mean dealing in horses, of course, my innocent Cockney brat, as I called you once before if you remember! Well, shall we try trotting now?'

We tried, and Arab trotted beautifully. As for me, I bumped

up and down madly, trying hard to look as if I were enjoying it, and not to show how precarious I felt.

'G-gosh! The s-saddle's a b-bit s-slippery, isn't it?' I gasped. Then all at once something happened. I caught the rhythm of the trot, and the world became smooth again.

'Sebastian!' I yelled. 'I've got it! I can trot!'

But alas! I had rejoiced too soon. Before my yell of triumph had died away, I had lost the rise and fall, and was once more bumping up and down like a cork on a rough sea, or a pea in a bottle.

'Gosh! Riding isn't as easy at it looks,' I said ruefully when we came to a steep hill and were walking the ponies.

'No, it isn't – like most other things,' answered Sebastian. 'Playing a violin looks as easy as falling off a log until you try to do it. So does ploughing a field. And I expect your dancing isn't as easy as it looks, either, is it?'

My thoughts flashed back to Madame's studio in Baker Street, and I remember how much practice it took to learn to do even a single *pirouette* well. I thought of my very first dancing lessons and how difficult it had seemed to do a simple *plié* properly.

'Turn out from ze 'ips. From ze 'ips I said, Veronique – not on-lee from ze feets. Ah, but do not displace ze 'ips; zat one must do nevaire. Keep ze 'eels on ze floor, leetle one. Now with ze music begin! One – two – three! Turn out from ze 'ips! Stop! You are bending ze back. Ze back – he must be straight, straight! Not bent like a bow. Now once again – one – two – three!—'

'No – it isn't easy,' I agreed.

'By the way, Veronica,' Caroline said curiously – we had got to the top of the hill by this time and Fiona, having emerged from the sulks, was waiting for us – 'what is an – whatever it is that your pony's named after?'

I laughed.

86

'Oh, you mean an *arabesque*? It's like this . . .' I slipped my feet out of the stirrups and slid carefully off Arab's back. 'I'll show you.'

There in the middle of the deserted country road I demonstrated an *arabesque*, balancing on one leg and raising the other to form a line with my outstretched arm. Madame had once said that my *arabesque* had 'a good line', but now out here in the hot blue air with the young larch trees standing knee-deep in bracken, and the ring-doves cooing lazily from the depths of a little fir plantation by the side of the road, I felt that she'd have been even more pleased with my *arabesque* could she have seen it today. The beauty all around me did something to me inside. I can't describe what it was, but it made me want to turn my *arabesque* into something better than it had been before. I wanted to express in my dancing the lovely effect of the sunlight flickering through the trees in the wood, the delicate green of the larches, the grace of the fox-gloves growing on the Roman Wall that marched side by side with the road just here.

'Oh! – *lovely*!' breathed Caroline. 'I didn't know your dancing was like that, Veronica.'

Sebastian said nothing, but his blue eyes met mine, full of understanding and admiration.

'I think it's perfectly silly,' came Fiona's voice, shattering my dream. 'The silliest thing I ever saw in my life – standing on one leg like a stork!' She dug her heels into her pony's flanks, and dashed away up the road as if the foul fiend was after her.

'Funny how different people like doing different things,' Sebastian said thoughtfully as he helped me to mount my pony again. 'That's what Fiona likes doing – charging about the countryside with a horse under her to do all the work. Some people' – he carefully didn't say himself, I noticed – 'like playing five-finger exercises on the piano, or scraping with a

I dreamt I'd been accepted for Sadler's Wells Ballet

bit of catgùt on another bit of catgut, and making harrowing noises. Now Caroline—'

'I like cooking,' Caroline said promptly. 'I'm going to be a cook when I grow up. Imagine being able to cook anything you like to eat! I'd make chocolate éclairs for lunch, tea, and dinner every day.'

Sebastian laughed.

'Golly! How sick you'd be after a week! Well, as I was saying, there's Veronica – she likes standing on one leg like a stork. Funny isn't it?'

'Yes,' I said rather vaguely. 'It is queer.' My thoughts had flown back again to that Baker Street studio with its polished floors and mirrors, and the *barres* along the walls. In my imagination I could hear the music – Handel's *Water Music* that Madame's pianist always played for some of the exercises – and Madame's voice saying in her funny broken English:

'One and two and three and four and! ... Stretch ze feet, leetle one. Stretch till it hurt! Point ze toes beau-ti-fully, so! Zat is right! Once again. One and two and three and four and! ... Turn and repeat on ze uzzer side. Begin! ...'

That night I dreamt I'd been accepted for Sadler's Wells Ballet School, and that it was my very first day there. Quite clearly I saw in my dream the portico, and the plate beside the door with '45 Colet Gardens' upon it.

When I woke up my dream was still so vivid that I could hardly believe I was still here in Northumberland, and not in London hurrying off to my ballet class.

I determined to begin practising again that very day.

Part Two

The Dream Comes True

Chapter 1

A Year Later

It was the end of July – not the same July as the one when I had sat miserably in the Flying Scotsman on my way north, but exactly a year later. I wasn't sitting in a train this time, but in the Scotts' palatial car, and Fiona and Caroline and Aunt June were there too. We were haring smoothly along the white country road towards Newcastle, the reason being the school prize-giving and breaking-up. This was the usual sort of affair – a cross between a concert and a lecture, the concert provided by us, all in white dresses; the lecture by the head mistress, backed up by the celebrity who had been roped in to present the prizes. The prizes, by the way, were the sort of books no one in his right mind would read – like *Coleridge, Poetry and Prose, Bacon's Essays* or somebody's *Anthology of English Verse*. Nothing decent like the latest ballet book, or a book on horses, or even as Caroline said, a cookery book. No wonder we sat in the car feeling gloomy!

As I sat there, I thought of the past year, and all that had happened in it. I'd learned to ride for one thing, and now I was nearly as keen on ponies as my cousins were. We still had Arabesque, by the way. When the eight weeks were up and we'd taken him back to Merlingford, Mr Tompkinson had shot a look at him and said that he certainly *was* improved with all the grooming we'd given him, and that we could go on keeping him a bit longer for nothing, if we liked – in fact, until he wanted him. Well, so far he hadn't wanted him, and as Sebastian said: 'Sufficient unto the day is the evil thereof.' I'm not sure whether this is Shakespeare or the Bible, but it's a jolly good motto!

At the end of last summer holidays, the gloomy question of school arose as was to be expected. It had been settled at last by my going to the same day school in Newcastle as Fiona and Caroline. It took me at reduced fees because I was a clergyman's daughter, and an orphan at that. I was to leave at the end of this term and go to a boarding school that specialized in clergymen's children. I tried hard not to think of it. For one thing, I'd grown quite fond of the Newcastle school (despite the footling prizegivings), and for another and much greater reason – I knew that boarding school spelt death to my dreams of a dancing career. You can't train to be a ballet dancer at a clergy boarding school!

And then my dancing . . . From the day when I'd done that *arabesque* in the middle of the road until now, I'd practised faithfully – mostly in the big, nursery bathroom, with the towel-rail as a *barre*. It had worked out very well, especially in the winter, as the rail was heated! I'd worn a bare patch on the linoleum underneath the rail, which puzzled Trixie quite a bit, as of course *she* didn't know about my practising; in fact no one did. I always wedged a chair under the handle of the door when I was supposed to be having my bath, because as I have explained before, there wasn't a key. I'm afraid my baths were a bit sketchy in consequence.

The centre exercises – *pirouettes*, *arabesques*, *attitudes*, and things, I did in the bathroom too, rolling back the bathmat for the job. I did the *pointe*-work there as well. The things that took a lot of space – like *glissades grands-jetés*, ordinary *grands-jetés*, *full-contretemps*, *déboullés*, *cabroilés*, *jetés portés de côté*, and suchlike I did in the morning-room when I was supposed to be practising my music. I asked Aunt June if I might use the gramophone – I think she imagined I wanted to listen to chamber music, or symphony concerts, or something of the kind; anyway she said yes, and handed over to me a pile of records that someone had given to her, and that she didn't like. When I looked through them, I found to my joy a recording of Chopin's waltzes – the ballet music from *Les Sylphides*, and two or three from Delibes' *Coppélia*, besides the whole of Tchaikovsky's *Lac des Cygnes*. I had a grand time with them! I practised the Waltz from *Les Sylphides*, that Madame had taught me, until the record was quite worn out. Now I only put it on when I was feeling especially happy, because very soon you wouldn't be able to hear it at all! Needless to say, I always locked the door during my music practice too. Caroline didn't seem to mind, but Fiona was rude about it. Fortunately she came to the conclusion that I played so badly that I didn't want anyone to hear me, and after this I was left in peace.

When I'd plucked up courage and asked Aunt June if I could have some dancing lessons, she hadn't been nearly as awkward as I'd feared. It appeared that Fiona and Caroline went to an expensive dancing school in Newcastle where they learned to dance gracefully and take part in displays, wearing wonderful dresses, so really Aunt June couldn't very well refuse me my one weekly lesson with Miss Martin. It cost me one guinea a term, whereas Caroline and Fiona's lessons were four and a half guineas a term each. I got the idea that Aunt June wasn't exactly sorry to grant me my wish about going to Miss Martin. It was obvious that both Caroline and Fiona were going to cost their parents a lot of money in the near future. Fiona was to go to Harrogate College next term, and after that to a finishing school in Switzerland; Caroline was to go to Roedean soon afterwards.

'It's really refreshing to find young people wanting anything cheap nowadays,' she had said with a shrug when we'd been discussing the matter.

'Oh, Aunt June – I can pay for my lessons myself,' I said eagerly. 'I've got the money – honestly I have.' It was true; I still had the five pounds that Mrs Crapper and the people on the other floors had given me 'to buy something to remember them by'. I have an idea that Jonathan had given most of it. Incidentally the five pounds had risen to five pounds two and six through being in the post office.

Aunt June answered that she wouldn't hear of my paying for my own lessons. There was a reasonable amount of money for my education, so I could keep my pocket money to buy something else with. In some ways Aunt June was very decent.

I didn't argue, merely making a mental resolution to go on keeping my money in the post office so that it would get still more interest. I had an idea that I'd need it some day to buy shoes and tights with, and perhaps even a ballet dress.

Well, I had gone to my lesson with Miss Martin once a week. It was every Monday, and it wasn't till half past four, which was very convenient because we had to stay in town until a quarter to six, when Uncle John finished at his office. Then he brought us home with him in the car.

I discovered that Miss Martin had another class on Thursdays; it was a children's class, and she tried hard to persuade some of her students to stay for it, so that the kids would have people more advanced than themselves to copy, but none of them would. I volunteered for the job, and Miss Martin was so pleased that she offered to let me join in her Friday class as well, free of charge, as a reward. So now I had three lessons a week, though to be sure one of them was rather elementary. As they were all after school, in the time when we were just waiting about for Uncle John, I told Fiona and Caroline that I was going to Miss Martin's studio for a bit, and they thought I was just going there to practise. I'm afraid is sounds a bit deceitful, but I couldn't help it. I stilled my conscience by telling myself it wasn't as if I were actually doing something wrong, or hurting anybody in any way. After all, it was my precious career that was at stake, and I knew quite well that I couldn't possibly hope to become a ballet dancer on only one lesson a week.

Miss Martin said she'd had a letter about me from Madame, but she didn't tell me what was in it. When I unfolded to her my secret ambition, and asked her not on any account to give me away to Aunt June, she just smiled her little secret smile, which was one of the most attractive things about her, and said she'd do her best for me.

For my classes I still wore the old black tights and tunic I'd had in London. The tights were so much darned it was difficult to tell where the darn stopped and the tights began! The tunic was getting a bit moth-eaten, too. I was quite well off for shoes, as Stella, the girl who was at the Wells, had given me all the pairs she'd outgrown. I carefully stiffened the blocked ones when they went soft with some marvellous stuff Miss Martin told me about – shellac and methylated spirit.

But I must get back to the car. We were nearing Newcastle by this time, and in a very short while we were in the school hall listening to Miss Glover, our head mistress, telling an appreciative audience of parents and friends how well the school had done during the past year. Little bursts of clapping accentuated her remarks, for instance when she mentioned about Audrey Mason getting her scholarship to Cambridge, and Primula Smith being awarded a special travelling scholarship. I wondered if they would mention the fact when I danced the Lilac Fairy in *The Sleeping Beauty*, or took the lead in *Lac des Cygnes*. Looking at Miss Glover. I thought it unlikely, to say the least!

After the presentation of prizes and certificates, which didn't interest me much because I hadn't won any, there was the usual concert – if you could call it that. There was the head girl's recitation, all in Latin; a scene from *Peer Gynt* by the sixth form; several terribly dull duets for two pianos by music pupils; a violin solo by a girl who squeaked frightfully, and, last but not least, a French play by our form – the Fifth. I was a waiter, and all I had to say was 'Monsieur?' in an interrogating voice. So that didn't weigh on my mind very much, and I was able to think about the Lilac Fairy all through it. In fact I was so busy in my imagination doing my curtsy on Covent Garden stage that I very nearly forgot I was in the school hall and missed my cue!

After this, there was a cup of tea and a cake for the parents and friends, and lemonade and a biscuit for us. At five o'clock it was all over, and we were free to go home. I realized with a queer sinking feeling in my inside that the holidays had begun and that I was saying a final goodbye to the school I had grown to love.

After I had said farewell to several mistresses and girls who were my special friends, I packed all my books and shoes and other things into the car, which was waiting outside, and rushed round to Miss Martin's studio to say goodbye to her, because dancing school was finished too. When it began again in the autumn I wouldn't be there, alas!

Luckily it was only a few minutes from the school. When I got there, I found that Miss Martin had a visitor, and to my surprise it was Aunt June!

'Miss Martin asked me to call,' she explained, seeing my startled face. 'She wanted to discuss your career with me. Miss Martin thinks you dance rather well, Veronica; she wonders how you'd like to be a dancing mistress?'

'Oh, but . . .' I began in a horror-stricken voice. Then I met Miss Martin's eyes – far-seeing grey eyes they were, and there was an expression in them that I couldn't fathom. But I understood enough just to keep quiet and let Aunt June go on talking, which she did without any help from either of us.

'Miss Martin thinks you'd make an excellent dancing teacher, Veronica. Of course it's not *my* idea of a career for a girl. Still, it's not as if you were going on the stage.' Aunt June said this as if the stage was something disgraceful – not to be mentioned in polite society! 'And after all,' she went on, 'you certainly don't show much aptitude for anything else. I understand from Miss Stanley, your form mistress, that she'll be greatly surprised if you've passed your School Certificate. And judging by the reports of the other mistresses, you don't show a great deal of promise in any special subject. All except your drawing, and that I understand Miss Lishman, the art mistress, thinks "extraordinary". I'm not quite sure what she means by that word.'

I couldn't help smiling, because I knew exactly what Miss Lishman meant. I remembered my first lessons. Miss Lishman had looked rather puzzled over my drawing – I seemed to do things so much bigger than anyone else. Finally she asked me where I'd learnt, and what sort of paper I'd been used to drawing on.

'Oh, I've never learnt drawing,' I explained. 'But I used to watch Jonathan. He was an artist who lived on the floor above us and he was a great friend of Daddy's. I used to paint in oils mostly, on the backs of Jonathan's old canvases – the ones he hated. Sometimes, though, I used brown paper.'

'Brown paper?' echoed Miss Lishman in a startled voice.

'Oh, yes, done with size it's quite good for oils, and – it's marvellous for pastel drawing, you know. Then sometimes Jonathan gave me some sugar-paper—'

'I see,' said Miss Lishman doubtfully, and not a bit as if she

97

did. 'Well, I'm afraid we haven't any of those things here. You'll have to make do with ordinary drawing paper.' She handed me a piece of cartridge paper. It was about eight inches square and looked to me like a postage stamp.

'Oh, and sometimes Jonathan and I used to draw on the walls,' I went on, thoughts crowding in upon me. 'Friezes and things. We did a perfectly marvellous one of Bacchus riding on an ostrich, and all his followers in the most ridiculous attitudes. When we got tired of the things we drew, we just painted them out and did some more on top. We kept Bacchus for ages though. Jonathan said he was the only bright spot in the gloom of a London fog! He said it cheered him up no end to look at that ostrich, and realize what funny shapes animals have—'

'That will do, Veronica,' said Miss Lishman firmly, cutting me short. 'That seems to me to be a very queer way of drawing.'

I felt like saying that to paint a still-life consisting of a large pottery jug, draped with a violet curtain, a flower vase full of nasturtiums, at least a pound of tomatoes, several oranges, not to mention a large grapefruit – well, to paint all this on a bit of paper eight inches square seemed queer to *me*. But I didn't say so because it might have sounded rude. Anyway, I didn't consider the point worth arguing about. I did the painting, and I must say it was frightfully bad. Jonathan would have had a fit if he'd seen it!

It was after this lesson that I'd heard Miss Lishman use the word 'extraordinary'. She was talking to another mistress at the time.

I dragged my thoughts back from the drawing and tried to listen to what Aunt June was saying.

'Of course it will rather alter our plans for you – educationally, I mean. As Miss Martin says, you'll have to stay on at school here in Newcastle, so that you can go in for your dancing exams with her. And of course you'll have to have extra dancing lessons . . .'

Then I understood the look in Miss Martin's eyes!

She knew as well as I did what boarding school meant, and she was determined to save me from it. The careers of dancing teacher and ballet student march side by side for quite a long time, and who knew what might happen before their ways divided?

'Oh, Miss Martin!' I gasped, when Aunt June had gone on her dignified way, telling me to follow her in a very few minutes. 'Oh, Miss Martin, you *are* a darling! I see now why you wanted to talk about me to Aunt June. I see it all!' Then I'm afraid I forgot that Miss Martin was my dancing mistress. I put my arms round her and hugged her and Miss Martin hugged me back. That's the best of dancing mistresses – they're not like the mistresses in ordinary schools. They're much more human. I certainly can't imagine anyone hugging Miss Glover, not even if they'd just passed their School Certificate with seven credits!

'But you understand of course, Veronica,' Miss Martin said when we were both calm again, 'that if, when the time comes, your aunt won't let you take up dancing – professionally, I mean – you'll have to give in and teach, you know.' Then, seeing my downcast face, she added cheerfully: 'After all, my dear, teaching dancing is a good life. I've done it for a long time and been very happy – perhaps happier than I'd have been on the stage, though I don't expect you to see it like that just now. In any case, I'm quite sure you'd rather teach dancing than, say, Latin or domestic science, wouldn't you?'

'Oh, yes – *rather*!' I agreed fervently.

'Then I think we've done the right thing,' went on Miss Martin. 'And for the present you must work hard. There's your Elementary RAD exam* – you haven't passed it yet, you

* Royal Academy of Dancing

know. Of course you're a long way beyond it now, but you'll still have to take it. And that reminds me' – she broke off, and went over to a tall cupboard where the best fancy costumes were kept – 'Mrs Grantly brought this in' – she held up a most gorgeous *tutu*. With its snowy frills of tarlatan it made me think of the corolla of a beautiful white flower. 'Marigold has outgrown it. Poor Marigold! I'm afraid she's going to be too big for ballet. Her mother thought I might find someone who would like to buy it. She wants fifteen shillings for it. That seems to me a great bargain.'

'I should just think it is!' I exclaimed. 'Why a *tutu* like that, new, would cost the earth! Can I buy it, Miss Martin? I've got loads of money of my very own. Several pounds, anyway.'

'That what I thought,' smiled Miss Martin. 'You'll need it for your exam at Christmas.'

'Will I go to London for it?' I questioned, thinking of dear Mrs Crapper, and Jonathan, and all my other friends. '*Couldn't* I please go to London for it, Miss Martin? It's really not much farther than Edinburgh, is it?'

'Just a few miles!' teased Miss Martin. 'Well, perhaps we might manage it. If you take it in London, it will have to be in January. That might be just as well, after all; it will give you more time to work on the syllabus.'

'Oh, *thank* you!' I said with a gasp of joy. Although I had grown to love beautiful Northumberland dearly, London was still my home. Even to think of the Tube, and Trafalgar Square with its pigeons, Piccadilly Circus with Eros poised ready to take flight, made me feel quivery in my inside. 'Thank you, Miss Martin. Thank you for everything, I *will* work hard.'

I ran down the stairs from the studio and out into the street, clasping the precious frock to my breast like a baby.

'Goodness!' I said aloud. 'I hope I haven't kept Aunt June

waiting. Golly! – I'm awfully sorry!'

The person I had collided with extricated himself from the ballet dress, and began to laugh.

'Veronica! Why the hurry?'

'Sebastian!' I yelled. 'I always seem to barge into you! I thought you didn't break up until tomorrow.'

'Chap in our form got chicken-pox,' Sebastian explained. 'Awful spot of luck – with the accent on the spot! The Powers-That-Be thought it wisest to pack us all off home, as it was so near the end of term.'

'That doesn't mean that you'll be in quarantine?' I asked anxiously.

'Good Lord, no! I've had the foul D spelt F-O-W-L – *dis*-ease!' laughed Sebastian. 'Not a snag anywhere, I assure you! In other words, everything in the garden's lovely! But what's all this?' – he pointed to the mass of white tarlatan in my arms. 'Are you taking home the laundry, or something?'

'Idiot! It's my new ballet frock,' I explained. 'Oh, Sebastian – I'm getting there! Really, I am. Aunt June says I'm to be a dancing teacher—'

Sebastian's brow puckered. 'But I thought—'

'Oh, yes – I know what you're thinking,' I burst out. 'But you're wrong. Of course I'm not *really* going to be a dancing teacher, but Aunt June thinks I am. It's the thin end of the wedge, if you see what I mean. I'll try to win Aunt June over later on, and you bet I'll do it!'

'Aunt June . . .' Sebastian said thoughtfully. 'Does that mean she's here, in town?'

'Oh, yes. She's just round the corner, at school,' I said. 'You see it's breaking-up day, and we've had a prize-giving and all that stuff. Ghastly! And by the way, she'll be waiting for me in the car. I must simply *dash*! What about you? How are you getting home? Why not come with us – there's loads of room?'

'What? With Aunt June and Cousin Fiona, not to mention

101

the obsequious Perkins?' laughed Sebastian. 'And I suppose the sumptuous Rolls? Not for this child! Couldn't stand it – altogether too_ overpowering! Besides, I have quite a few things I want to do in town. No, I'll come back in the homely bus. Fortunately this is Tuesday -- Market Day!'

Our eyes met and we laughed. Sebastian still lost no opportunity of teasing me about my sad attempt at running away.

'D'you know,' I said, 'I've never realized it before, but if you and Fiona and Caroline are cousins, then you must be a sort of cousin of mine, too, Sebastian.'

'Sort of,' agreed Sebastian. 'But only sort of, if you know what I mean. Different side of the family. Well, I'll be getting along. See you tonight most likely – provided I don't miss the bus. So long, Cousin Veronica-sort-of, dancing-teacher elect!' He swung himself on to a passing trolley-bus, waved his school cap gaily, and in another moment his teasing face was lost to view in a maze of traffic.

I went on my way somewhat more soberly, but my heart was singing with joy at the wonderful thing that had happened to me.

Chapter 2

The Holidays Begin

We didn't see Sebastian that night after all. When seven o'clock came and he still hadn't arrived, we rang up the lodge to see what had happened. Bella McIntosh, the woman from the village, who'd looked after Sebastian and his father ever since Sebastian's mother had died five years ago, answered our ring. She told us that only a few minutes ago Sebastian himself had rung up from Newcastle, saying that he'd met his father in town, and that they were doing a show. He also said that, if we rang up, Bella was to say that he was very sorry about tonight, but he couldn't make it.

'Well!' Fiona said, putting down the receiver. 'What do you think of that? Going to a show when *we're* here waiting for him. And after telling Veronica he would see us tonight—'

'He said he *expected* he'd see us,' I put in, determined to be fair to Sebastian. 'But, after all, if his father wanted him to go to a show, well, Sebastian could hardly insist on dashing back here, just to be with us for nothing in particular, now could he?'

'Yes,' he could,' Fiona retorted. 'After he'd *promised*.'

I said no more. It was never any use arguing with Fiona. Instead, I retired to the bathroom and did an hour's practising, and after this it was time for bed.

Next morning I got up early as usual and practised before breakfast. After breakfast I locked myself into the morning-room by sheer force of habit, and practised scales and exercises conscientiously for half an hour, and did centre-work for another half. After which I felt free to join the others and share in their plans. Miss Martin said that an hour and a half's work a day was enough for anyone to do during the holidays.

I crashed round to the stables where I guessed the others would be. Fiona was rubbing Melisande down with a silk hankie, and Caroline was out in the field trying to round up Arab and Warrior – she'd already caught Gillyflower, she told me.

'Right-ho! You leave Arab to me!' I yelled back. 'I can get him easily with a lump of sugar. He always falls for it.'

'Not with me he doesn't!' grumbled Caroline. 'I've used up nearly half a pound on him. He always snatches it, and then dashes off just when you're going to grab him.'

'Watch me!' I answered, stealing up to my pony with the sugar on my outstretched palm. 'Come along, old boy!'

Sure enough, Arab allowed himself to be caught. I expect he knew that I was his mistress and Caroline only my understudy, so to speak, because the same thing always happened whenever *I* tried to catch Gillyflower for her. He just wouldn't let me get near him.

'Gosh! This is a hopeless job!' poor Caroline panted, as she stood in the middle of the field, hands on hips, watching Warrior charge round, head up, tail streaming. 'I do wish Sebastian would turn up and catch his own beastly pony!'

Just as the words left her lips, there was a shout, and Sebastian took a flying leap over the fence into the field.

'I've just been calling your pony names!' yelled Caroline. 'I've been chasing him round this field for *hours* – ten minutes, anyway. I'm through!'

OK!' laughed Sebastian. 'Gosh! He's fat, isn't he? I'll bet you lot haven't been exercising him as you promised you would while I was away at school.'

'We did try,' Caroline said apologetically. 'But he's so awful to catch for anyone except you, Sebastian, and Fiona—'

'Oh, I know all about Fiona! *She* wouldn't do a fellow a good turn if she could help it—'

'I didn't mean that—'

'Maybe not,' drawled Sebastian. 'But it's true, all the same.' Unfortunately Fiona was standing at the stable door and had heard everything. I have an idea that Sebastian meant her to hear.

'Of course dear Veronica was no end of a help,' Fiona said scoffingly. 'She rode Warrior every day for you, Sebastian!'

Sebastian stared back at her scornfully.

'You *are* a little cat!' he stated. 'You know very well that Veronica isn't up to Warrior yet. By the way, how's the riding coming on, Veronica?'

'Oh, I like it no end,' I assured him. 'But then anyone would like riding Arab – he's so good-mannered. He never takes nips at me like Melisande does when Fiona isn't looking, or bucks me off—'

'No – he's a nice animal,' agreed Sebastian. 'Well, I'll be off to catch my steed. See you later!'

We walked back into the stable, and I began to groom Arab.

'If you want Sebastian to like you, you won't make him do it by saying unkind things about Veronica,' Caroline observed.

'Who said I wanted him to like me?' flashed Fiona. 'I don't care in the least whether he likes me or not. I think he's detestable!'

'When people keep on saying other people are detestable, it makes you think they rather like them!' stated Caroline.

In less than no time, Sebastian was with us, leading Warrior by the forelock.

'I vote we go for a ride this afternoon,' he said as he rubbed him down with a dandy-brush. 'Let's go right up on to the moors. You don't know how I've been longing for a ride ever since half-term. Let's have a picnic on Corbie's Nob. We

105

haven't been there for ages and ages – two years, I should think.'

'Oh, but Sebastian,' Fiona said, 'there's a tennis party over at the Frazers – Lingfield, you know. I've promised to go, and I said you'd go too. They'll be expecting you—'

'What? Me go to a sticky tennis party at the Frazers on the first day of the hols. Not jolly likely!' Sebastian said. 'Anyway, by rights we shouldn't have broken up until today, so they can't be expecting me.'

'I told them you'd be home by lunchtime, and the party doesn't begin until three o'clock, so there'd still have been loads of time,' argued Fiona. 'And you're my partner—'

'*Your* partner?' Sebastian retorted. 'Oh, no – think again! I'm not anyone's partner. I'm going riding—'

'But I shall be without a partner—'

'Well, that's your fault. You shouldn't go including me in your rash promises. I like to be *asked* when I'm going to do a thing.'

'But I *can't* go without a partner,' wailed Fiona. 'Oh, Sebastian – you *might* be obliging just for once.'

'I'm not obliging,' said Sebastian. 'Never was! Anyway, you don't oblige *me*. What about that pony? You never exercised him once for me.'

He went on imperturbably grooming Warrior, whilst Fiona stood in the doorway with clenched hands.

'Are you going to come?'

'No, I'm not. I've told you – I'm going riding.'

'You're perfectly beastly!' exclaimed Fiona, seeing that Sebastian was not to be moved. 'I told Caroline you were, and it's true. Since Veronica came, you—'

Sebastian's imperturbability vanished. He snatched up his riding-crop from where it lay on the window-sill.

'Just one more word in that strain . . .' he threatened.

Fiona didn't know whether he was serious, and neither did

we, but she evidently thought that discretion was the better part of valour, for she said no more, but dashed out of the stable like a whirlwind, flung herself upon Melisande's back, and was away.

'Well, I suppose that means we don't include *her* in our plans,' Caroline said as she picked up her brushes and things and put them into her bag. 'Even if she's out of the tennis, she certainly won't come with us. Sebastian you *are* naughty! You always rub Fiona up the wrong way!'

'I like that! She always rubs *me* up the wrong way. Me be her partner at tennis? The very idea! Why, I'd have to do every spot of the work and then take all the blame when we lost! I know all about Fiona and her tennis! And without as much as a "Will you?" let alone a "please".'

'Corbie's Nob? That's the peak you can see from the ponies' field, isn't it?' I put in, anxious to take Sebastian's thoughts away from Fiona. 'Can we ride all the way?'

'Every step,' Sebastian replied. 'Except for the very top. I know all the gates, and the gaps in the walls, and everything. We go across Three Tree Moor and then up on to the Nob. It's a stiffish climb, but it's worth it when you get to the top. You can see three counties and right over into Bonnie Scotland on a clear day.'

'Let's collect up the stuff for the picnic now,' suggested Caroline. 'Then we'll be able to start off straight after lunch. I saw Trixie making some girdle scones – let's beg some.'

'Girdle scones,' mused Sebastian. 'Gosh! They sound good! When you're away at school you forget there are such things.'

Chapter 3

Corbie's Nob

Fiona regarded us scornfully as we loaded ourselves with eatables and drinkables ready for our climb. She herself was arrayed in spotless tennis finery – white silk pleated shorts-frock, snowy shoes and ankle socks. Under her arm she carried a Slazenger tennis racket.

'Won't you be rather the worse for wear?' Sebastian asked innocently, buckling Warrior's girths, and pulling down his stirrup irons. 'I mean, after you've ridden all the way over to Lingfield in those togs?'

'I'm not going to ride,' Fiona told him loftily.

Sebastian gave a whistle.

'Gosh! You don't mean to say you're going to trek there – leg it – shanks' pony? Who would have thought it?'

'I'm going by car, of course,' Fiona said. 'Any objection?'

Sebastian shrugged his shoulders. The look on his expressive face told Fiona more clearly than any words exactly what he meant. 'Fancy going to play tennis in a *car*,' that look said. 'I knew it would be a sticky party!'

'Well, so long!' he said, swinging himself into the saddle. 'Ready, you two? Then let's be off. By the way, Fiona, don't forget that the super-charged tennis racket you hold beneath your arm is to do more than make everyone at the party jealous!' With which parting thrust he was away before Fiona had time to reply, we following close on his heels.

We rode out into the North Meadow where Fiona's pony was grazing – Fiona had turned her out before she went off for her tennis. As we cantered across the short grass, Melisande charged round on her own, tail streaming. Every now and then she would stop to snort. When we left the field by the gate on the far side, she looked after us longingly and whinnied, her ears pricked. We did feel mean, leaving her behind.

'It's Fiona's fault,' Caroline said. 'She oughtn't to have wanted to go to a stupid tennis party on the very first day of the hols.'

'Of course tennis is OK,' Sebastian observed. 'Don't think I despise a game of tennis – far from it. But a spot of tennis here among ourselves, where you can get a decent game, is one thing, and a sticky party at the Frazers, all dolled up, is quite another.'

After this none of us said anything for quite a bit. The going was hard, and we were fully occupied urging our ponies onwards and upwards through the shoulder-deep bracken that encircled the lower slopes of Three Tree Moor like a huge girdle. When we had got above the bracken the going was easier. Here the fell was covered with short heather and out-crops of rock with now and then stretches of sheep-nibbled turf. Leading away in all directions were the narrow, ribbon-like tracks made by the sheep.

Up and up we climbed, the air seeming to become more hot and blue every minute. And then, suddenly, we breasted the brow of the fell, and saw Three Tree Moor before us – a lonely expanse of rock-strewn turf with another steep ascent on the far side.

'Oh!' I said disappointedly, gulping down draughts of the cool mountain air that blew across the moor. 'I thought Corbie's Nob was on top of here.'

Sebastian laughed.

'That's always the way when you're making for a peak. It's always just over the top of the next slope, and then when you get there, sure as anything you find there's still another one to climb. I should say there are quite three more before we get to the Nob. Take a dekko at the jolly old Hall and surroundings because you won't be able to see them again till you get on top of the Nob.'

We dismounted and sat on the edge of the steep, heathery hillside, letting the ponies graze on a patch of turf nearby. We knew they'd be easy enough to catch when we wanted them – the climb had sobered them down considerably.

Everything was so quiet up here that you could hear the sheep nibbling, and the bees taking the honey from the heather all around us. While we'd climbed upwards, several peewits had collected and had flown round us in circles, uttering their plaintive cries. But now even these had flown away, and the silence was unbroken unless you could count umpteen larks, so high up in the blue air that they were quite invisible. Their song was so continuous that in time it became part of the silence. Occasionally a curlew, with long curving beak, flew languidly over our heads, startling the ponies by its shrill cry of alarm, so different from the lovely notes it utters when it rises from the ground into the sky.

Far below us lay Bracken Hall looking incredibly small and neat. Tiny fields lay spread out around it like pocket handkerchiefs, and in one of them a little animal we knew to be Melisande cropped at the grass. The lake glittered like a jewel with a crescent of sombre fir woods for its setting. Beyond the Hall lay the little village of Bracken with its square-towered church, and a glint of blue that Sebastian told us was the burn that flowed through it.

'Well, let's be getting on, shall we?' Sebastian said, when we had rested for a bit. 'We've still a good way to go. "Excelsior" as the highwayman said when they hung him on the gibbet.'

'Oh, Sebastian, but it wasn't ...' I began, when I saw the laughter in his blue eyes. 'Oh, I see – you were joking.'

'Lady, I never joke,' Sebastian assured me solemnly.

110

'May you be forgiven!' I retorted. 'You never do anything else – at least hardly ever,' I added, remembering the Sebastian I had met on that far-away railway journey.

When we got to the lower slopes of the Nob, we left the ponies at the bottom of the final ascent and started to climb on foot. The Nob was composed chiefly of black rocks that jutted out of a precipitous, shaly hillside, like raisins in a rock bun. On the top was a stone cairn.

'It marked a British Burial ground in the first place,' Sebastian panted, leaping upwards. 'Then the Borderers used it for a beacon turret to warn the other places round that the Scots were coming. Excelsior! Higher and still higher, and mind the snakes!'

'Snakes?' I gasped.

'Idiot!' panted Caroline. 'I mean *you*, Sebastian. Veronica thought you were serious.'

'Well, so I was,' answered Sebastian. 'There might be some. There are lots on the moors.'

'Only grass snakes—'

'Well, they're snakes, aren't they?'

'I suppose so, but they're quite harmless.'

'There are adders, too,' persisted Sebastian. 'I saw one the other day. A black one – they're deadly poisonous. I mean their bites are.'

'Oh, Sebastian – *where*?'

'In a bottle in the Jingling Gate Inn parlour,' Sebastian said with a grin. 'It was caught up here on the Nob fifty years ago.'

We breathed again.

Sebastian, you are a beast, frightening us like that!' Caroline exclaimed. 'My heart's going pit-a-pat.'

'I thought you wanted a thrill,' said Sebastian. 'So I provided one. Always the little gentleman, yours truly! Well, here we are. How's this for a view?'

We stood on the summit of the Nob and gasped, partly because of the exertion of our climb, but chiefly because of the beauty and wildness of the scene spread out before us. At our feet lay what looked like an uninhabited land of huge, rounded hills – the Cheviots, the Border country that lies between England and Scotland. To the north-west lay what looked like a dark, woolly carpet.

'That's the new forest the Forestry Commission has just planted,' Sebastian explained. 'It's going to be the biggest forest in England when they've finished. It's going to stretch right up to the Border. When it grows up, these hills won't look nearly so bare and desolate.'

When our eyes had got accustomed to the view, we were able to pick out villages and hamlets. We could even see a tiny puff of smoke that marked the little station of Deadwater.

'It always puzzles me why on earth they went and built a station at Deadwater, of all places,' mused Sebastian. 'There's nowhere to go to from here except the open fell. D'you see that misty, blue streak over to the east, between those two hills? That's the sea.'

'The sea?' we echoed excitedly. 'Just where will it be?'

'Oh, away up by Holy Island, I should say,' answered Sebastian. 'No, on second thoughts, it won't be as far north as that. It'll be somewhere round about Alnmouth, or Hauxley – the coast opposite Coquet Island, you know. It's hard to tell though. How about having our picnic up here?'

We all agreed that you couldn't get a better place for our meal. 'Come on, then! Walk up, walk up, ladies and gentlemen to see the lions fed!' Sebastian dislodged a big, flat stone from the side of the cairn for us to use as a table and we spread out our provisions.

'Apple cake, gingerbread, rock buns, sandwiches and, of course, Trixie's girdle scones,' I said, unwrapping the things Caroline and I had brought. 'What have you got, Sebastian?'

'Fruit cake, sausage rolls, and a jam tart,' he answered, handing them over to Caroline. 'I've got lemonade, too.'

'Golly!' Caroline exclaimed as she unpacked the things. 'The jam tart's got mixed up with the sausage rolls! Will it matter, do you think?'

'Oh, no – not at all,' Sebastian said airily. 'Improve them, I should say. Give 'em a unique flavour. We might try a dash of lemonade on them as well. *Sauce citronnade*. Sausages *à la* whatever-the-French-for-jam-is.'

'*Confiture*, of course,' I said.

'No "of course" in that superior manner, my child,' said Sebastian, his eyes snapping, 'or you won't get any! Well, as I was saying, sausages *à la confiture avec sauce citronnade*. Any offers?'

'No, thank you,' Caroline and I said both together. 'We prefer our sausage rolls *without* lemonade.'

'Just as you like,' said Sebastian with a wave of his hand. 'I'm always ready to pander to the common taste. You can have them *ordinaire* or whatever it is they call it. What's the matter, Veronica? You look struck all of a heap.'

'Did I? I was thinking, that's all.' I didn't volunteer to tell them what I was thinking but, as a matter of fact, I had once again noticed Sebastian's wonderful hands, and the way he used them to express himself. Most people talk with their voices; Sebastian did it with his hands. When he said 'No, you can't do that' he didn't just say it. He moved his hands, and they forbade you. I can't explain it, but that's how it was.

Meanwhile he had fished three cups out of his haversack and was pouring lemonade into them.

'Do you prefer your champagne dry, or the other thing?' he inquired.

'Dry?' I echoed. 'How on earth cane wine be *dry*?'

'Search me!' said Sebastian. 'But I assure you it can. All the best wine lists say so.'

'Well, what's the other thing?' I asked. 'Wet, I suppose? I think I'll have mine wet.'

'I've an idea it isn't wet,' Sebastian said. 'I've an idea it's – it's – dash it all, I can't think what it can be.'

'Well, never mind – let's all have it wet,' suggested Caroline.

And this is what we did. We held up our glasses – I mean cups – and drank toasts to all the people we knew. Most of them were perfectly idiotic toasts, but at the end, when there was only a drop of lemonade left in our glasses, the bantering look died out of Sebastian's eyes, and he said quite seriously: 'Here's to our secret – yours and mine, Veronica! May we both achieve our heart's desire.'

Of course Caroline wanted to know what the secrets were, and of course Sebastian refused to tell her.

'They wouldn't be secrets then, would they?' he teased.

'Well, I think you're terribly mean,' she grumbled. 'And anyway, you can't drink toasts to yourselves – it just isn't done.'

'Isn't it?' retorted Sebastian. 'Watch me!' So saying he clinked his glass against mine, said 'Here's to US, Veronica!' and finished the rest of the lemonade in one gulp.

After we had packed the cups and the sandwich paper back into the rucksacks, we hid the empty lemonade bottle in a crevice in the cairn, and climbed down from our rocky eyrie.

'Let's try to find some white heather while we're here, shall we?' said Sebastian. 'There used to be quite a big patch over to the right of that boggy ground. I remember getting some there once. White heather is very rare, you know,' he explained to me, 'and if you *do* find any, it's supposed to bring you good luck. That's what we both need just now, eh Veronica? A spot of real good luck.'

We looked and looked but although there were masses of bell heather in full bloom, and quite a lot of the ordinary just beginning to come out, not a trace of white did we see.

'Queer – I'll swear it was somewhere about here,' Sebastian declared as we squelched about in the boggy ground. We'd taken off our shoes for the job and I must say it was lovely to feel the cool, peaty mud oozing up between your toes. There were lots of marsh flowers growing on the bog. Sebastian explained that the little white ones, like tiny wind anemones, were called Grass of Parnassus.

'It doesn't grow in many places,' he added. 'Here and on Holy Island are the only ones I know. Pretty, isn't it?'

'Lovely,' I agreed.

'We'd better be making tracks,' he said, after we had squelched round for a long time, and come no nearer to finding anything that even faintly resembled white heather.

It was on our way back to the patch of grass where the ponies were grazing that the dreadful thing happened. We had picked our way over the boggy part, jumping from clump to clump of coarse grass so as to avoid sinking in knee-deep, and had got to where the rocks and heather began, when I felt a sudden pain shoot through my ankle. Looking down I saw something wriggle away into the heather, and disappear amongst an outcrop of rock – something long, and black, and sinister.

'Sebastian!' I yelled. 'Sebastian! Come quick! I've been bitten by something! It was a snake – I saw it!'

'Gosh!' Sebastian came rushing up, not bothering to step on the tufts of grass, but plunging through the bog all anyhow in his effort to reach me quickly. 'Golly! Are you sure?'

'Of course I'm sure!' I said, tears of fright springing to my eyes. 'You can see the mark. Look!'

I pointed down at my ankle and there, sure enough, was a small red mark like a scratch.

'Was it green – the thing that bit you, I mean?' Sebastian demanded. 'What was it like?'

'It wasn't green!' I yelled. 'It was b-black. It was a black adder—'

'Nonsense!' snapped Sebastian, but all the same I saw him go white under his tan. 'There aren't any black adders now.'

'You said you saw one—'

'Yes, in a bottle. It was caught fifty years ago. There hasn't been another one found since.'

'This might be the time,' I hiccuped. 'And it was here the last one was caught. You said so.'

Then Sebastian seemed to make up his mind. He suddenly became the serious boy I'd met in the train.

'Sit down,' he ordered curtly, 'I don't for a moment believe it was a black adder you saw, but just in case—' He took a penknife out of his pocket, and a box of matches.

'W-what are you going to do with your knife?' I asked anxiously.

'I'm going to sterilize it,' he answered, lighting a match and holding the blade in the flame. 'Now don't be scared. I won't hurt you – at least not much.'

When the blade had cooled, he took my ankle in one slim, strong hand and began to scratch the red mark with the knife until it began to bleed quite fast. Then he put his head down, and before I knew what he was about, he had placed his lips to the wound and was sucking it, spitting over his shoulder into the heather at intervals. I was so interested that I nearly forgot it was me that had been bitten!

'There now – I think that will do. If it *was* an adder, that ought to have put paid to his little game! As for black adders, I just don't believe it. All the same, we must get down quickly and find a house where we can get spirit of some sort.'

'What about the doctor?' said Caroline.

'Yes, I'd thought about him,' said Sebastian. 'But today is Wednesday, and it's his day at Depton. Goodness only knows where he'll be just now. Anyway, we must find somewhere

116

nearer than that. I know! Sandy Mactavish's cottage at the foot of the fell – Pasture Cottage, it's called. We'll make for it.'

'Why Sandy Mactavish?' Caroline asked, as he bandaged my ankle with a not-too-clean hankie he'd pulled out of his pocket.

'Red nose,' said Sebastian shortly.

'Red nose?' echoed Caroline in astonishment. 'What on earth has Sandy's nose got to do with Veronica's bite?'

'Whisky,' Sebastian said shortly. 'Best thing for snakebite. Sandy'll be sure to have some on hand – red nose. See?'

'You are clever,' Caroline said admiringly. 'I'd never have thought of that.'

The ride down to the little cottage at the foot of the fell was a nightmare. Every few minutes we kept stopping to have a look at my ankle just to reassure ourselves that it wasn't swelling. Every second or two Caroline or Sebastian kept asking me if I felt queer, or anything. When at last we arrived at the cottage and knocked on the door, I had begun to feel quite light-headed, though I know now that it wasn't snakebite, but only shock and imagination.

The door opened as if the person inside had been waiting for us on the mat, and a Scottish voice said: 'Weel?'

Sandy Mactavish was small and thin. He had red, tousled hair, small watery blue eyes, set close together, a long, thin mouth buttoned up tightly at the corners, and, of course, a red nose.

'Oh, Mr Mactavish – have you got a spot of whisky handy?' Sebastian said. Sebastian never wasted time in beating about the bush.

'Whusky?' echoed Mr Mactavish, with a startled look. 'Noo why should ye be thinking I'd hae the whusky in ma hoose?'

Sebastian's eyes strayed past Sandy Mactavish's shoulder to

117

the untidy room beyond, where, on a rough wood table, stood a dirty tumbler and a tell-tale bottle.

'Mebbie ye'll be telling me what bairns like ye'll be wanting wi' the whusky?' said Sandy, moving his shoulders so that it hid the table from our anxious eyes.

'Oh, don't worry – we don't want to *drink* it,' Sebastian assured him. 'We want to put it on Veronica's foot.' Then, seeing Sandy's outraged expression, he added: 'She's been bitten by a snake. We only want a spot – honestly. A teaspoonful will do.'

'Och aye,' said the Scotsman. 'Come awa in wi' ye, and a'll dee ma best for ye under the circumstances. Bitten by a snake ye say?'

He led the way into the dark kitchen, toddled over to a cupboard by the mantelpiece, took out a small medicine glass, and poured some liquid into it out of the bottle on the table. He held it up to the light for a second, then glanced at us.

'A teaspoonful ye said ye'd be wanting?'

'Och aye,' said Sebastian, with a glint of mischief in his eyes. 'If ye're sure ye can spare it.'

The man poured about half of the liquid back into the bottle; then he handed the glass to us.

'Then ye can hae that,' he said. 'And never let it be said that Sandy Mactavish didna dae what he could tae help a puir bit lassie in distress.'

Sebastian pushed me on to the one chair the room contained and unwound the handkerchief. Then he stood holding the medicine glass and looking down at me anxiously.

'I have an idea this will hurt like the dickens,' he said. 'Think you can stand it, Veronica?'

'I expect I can,' I said weakly.

'Well, here goes!' He poured the whisky on the wound gripping my foot tightly at the same time.

I gave a shriek.

'Ouch! It burns like anything!'

'It'll go off in a minute,' Sebastian assured me. And sure enough, after a second or two, the burning pain faded and I was able to smile.

'Puir lassie!' said a Scottish voice behind us – we'd almost forgotten Sandy in our agitation. 'Ye look awfu' white. Would ye no' like a cup o' tae, lassie?'

'Oh, *please*,' I answered gratefully. 'I would like a cup of tea most awfully.'

He went to the fireplace where a small, brown teapot stood on the hob, and poured some thick, black liquid into a cracked cup, added a drop of milk and some sugar, and brought it to me. Now that he knew his beloved whisky wasn't in danger, he was quite affable, was Sandy. I drank the stuff he brought me, and though it was anything but nice, it was hot and I felt better for it.

'Well, let's be getting on, shall we?' Sebastian suggested after he had replaced the bandage. 'Feel equal to riding, Veronica?'

'Yes – I think so,' I said feebly.

We had had to go some distance out of our way to reach Sandy's cottage, and now we found ourselves out on the moorland road that skirted the fell, running more or less east and west from Newcastle to the Border.

'We may as well go home this way, now,' said Sebastian. 'It'll be just as quick and much easier going.'

There was a wide grass verge to the road, and we could have cantered along it, but none of us felt like cantering. We walked soberly in single file, feeling anything but easy in our minds.

Suddenly there was a hoot from behind us and the sound of a car approaching.

'I wonder who it is?' Caroline said. I had learned by this time that, barring weekends, you usually knew all the cars and their occupants.

'Gosh! Of all the luck!' Sebastian yelled. 'Why, it's Dr Ridley! I know his car.'

'So it is!... Hi! Stop!...'

We pulled our ponies across the road and the car slid to a standstill.

'What's the matter now?' said the doctor, letting down the window and putting out his head.

Breathlessly we explained about the snakebite and immediately the doctor was all attention. In fact, before we'd finished our explanation he had switched off the car engine and was out of the car, bag in hand.

Once again the none-too-clean hankie was unwound and my foot scrutinized – this time minutely – the doctor firing off questions all the while.

Had I actually seen the snake? Had Sebastian or Caroline seen it? What colour was it? Did my foot hurt? Did it feel stiff? How did I feel myself?

'It was black,' I said firmly. 'The snake, I mean. And no one but me saw it. No, my foot doesn't hurt – except where Sebastian cut it.'

The doctor looked round at Sebastian questioningly.

'I sterilized the blade of my pocket-knife, sir,' Sebastian explained, 'and opened the wound to make it bleed. Then I sucked it good and hard.'

'Ah!' said the doctor, nodding his head. 'Good old-fashioned remedy, what!' Then he began to sniff. 'And what's this you've been putting on it, eh? Spirit?'

'Whisky,' said Sebastian. 'We got it at old Sandy Mactavish's – Pasture Cottage.'

'Yes – you'd get it there all right!' laughed the doctor. 'Trust old Sandy to have a spot of whisky about!' Then he turned to me. 'Well, young lady – there don't seem to be any symptoms of snakebite as far as I can see, but of course that may be due to the prompt action of Sebastian here. Couldn't

120

have done better myself under the circumstances. If there's the least swelling or pain in that foot, ring me up at once. I'm quite sure you can wash out any fears of a black adder. Most likely what you saw was a harmless grass snake.'

'But the pain?' I said. 'The scratch on my ankle?'

'Done by a sharp stone, or a bit of heather perhaps, and you imagined the rest. It's amazing what the imagination can do!' He dived back into his car, produced a roll of bandages, and did up my foot again rather more professionally. 'Well, I'll be getting along.'

'Just a jiffy!' said Sebastian, his foot on the running-board. 'You don't have to tell them at the Hall – I mean Aunt June and the rest – about all this, do you, Dr Ridley? They'd get into a flat spin—'

The doctor's eyes twinkled.

'I see how it is! You're afraid they might cut up rough and curtail your activities, eh? Well, I won't give you away, if Veronica's foot stays as it is now. You'd better ring me up tomorrow morning, all the same, just to let me know everything's all right.'

'I'll do that,' agreed Sebastian. 'I'll ring you up from our place.'

We watched the doctor's car disappear and then rode homewards ourselves, feeling much more cheerful.

'I'll bet that's what it was – just coincidence,' Sebastian declared, as the Hall chimneys came into view amongst the trees. 'The grass snake just happened to be there when you cut your foot, Veronica, so of course you thought it had bitten you – especially when we'd been talking about that black adder at the Jingling Gate.'

'It was *black*,' I insisted.

'Imagination,' retorted Sebastian, 'as Dr Ridley said.'

Well, we were never to know. The fact remained that my foot didn't swell, nor did I have any after-effects. But I still stuck to my point – that the snake I'd seen was a black snake. We were thankful that Dr Ridley was such an understanding sort of man, for we felt that if he'd given us away the grown-ups might easily have forbidden us to go out on to the moors alone. The fact that nothing had actually happened to me wouldn't weigh with them in the least. Grown-ups can be terribly unreasonable!

'By the way, Veronica,' Sebastian said, as we rode round to the stables, 'just when you gave that blood-curdling yell up there on the Nob, I found that patch of white heather. I clean forgot about it in the uproar! The patch is a lot smaller than it used to be, so perhaps that's why it took such a lot of finding. Also it isn't out yet, but it's white all right – I remembered the place when I found it again. So all's well that ends well! Here's your spot of good luck!' He took a sprig of heather out of his buttonhole – I'd been far too het up to notice it before – solemnly broke it in two, and handed the bigger piece to me.

We met Fiona in the hall. She looked as fresh and cool as if she'd never heard the word 'tennis' in her life.

'Did you have a good time?' Caroline asked.

'Oh, super!' Fiona said, regarding us distastefully. I must admit that we weren't exactly tidy! Sebastian had bits of heather in his hair; my leg was daubed with blood, and there was a distinct smell of whisky about me. Caroline's face was streaked with the tears she had shed, and she'd caught her cardigan on a gorse bush and pulled the stitches, which certainly didn't improve the look of it.

'I had a perfectly marvellous time,' went on Fiona. 'Ian Frazer was my partner, and I must say he was decently dressed – new flannels and everything.' She cast a sidelong glance at Sebastian to see how he took this world-shattering announcement.

'He *would*!' Sebastian answered. 'The little tick"

'Well, anyway, we won,' Fiona went on triumphantly. 'And

look what I got for a prize.' She proudly held out for our inspection a brooch made in the form of two crossed tennis rackets.

'Jolly nice!' I exclaimed. It really was an awfully attractive brooch. 'What did Ian get?'

'Oh, the boys' first prize was a tennis-racket press,' said Fiona. 'It was awfully lucky because Ian broke his press last week, so he was just wanting a new one.'

'So of course you won,' Sebastian said in a scornful voice. 'For obvious reasons!'

Caroline and I glanced at each other significantly. We both knew quite well what Sebastian meant. It was no secret that Ian Frazer was the world's worst cheat.

'I don't know what you mean,' declared Fiona. 'Ian's a jolly good player. I wouldn't have won if I'd played with you.'

'Not in that way you wouldn't!' Sebastian flashed. 'So isn't it a good thing I cried off?'

'Who was there?' Caroline asked quickly, seeing that things were getting strained. 'The Listers, I suppose?'

'Yes, Richard and Elizabeth were there. And David Eliot of Dewburn, and of course Patience. There were two girls called Moffit, and some cousins of theirs – Alan and Dick something or other. I forget their surname. Well, I think I'll go and change – it's nearly seven o'clock. You'd better do something to your face, Caroline,' she added. 'Trixie will have a fit if she sees you like that.' She sauntered off, and we looked after her.

'Yes, I expect she's right – I'd better have a wash,' Caroline said, after a glance in the hall mirror. 'Coming, Veronica?'

'In just a minute,' I answered. 'I must just have a look at my foot to see if it's still OK. You go on; shan't be long!'

'Why do you always rub Fiona up the wrong way?' I asked Sebastian, as I replaced the bandage, having satisfied myself that my ankle hadn't swollen. 'Why do you hate her so much?'

Sebastian raised his eyebrows.

'Didn't know I did hate her. Now you come to mention it, though, I suppose I do. She's so – so – what I mean to say is she's decent-looking, and she never forgets it, or lets anyone else forget it either. She goes about all day long looking at herself – oh, I don't mean in mirrors, though she does plenty of that, too. I just mean she's never thinking about anything else but herself and her stupid good looks. I'd give anything just to take that smug, self-satisfied look off her face! One day I'll do it! She infuriates me.'

'I see...' I stared at Sebastian curiously. There was no denying the fact that there was a queer streak in him. He either liked you or he didn't, and woe betide you if he didn't – there were no half-measures about Sebastian! Moreover, it seemed to me that his likes and dislikes had neither rhyme nor reason. He disliked Fiona and Aunt June and Uncle John. Well, I could understand that all right, because, after all, they were living in his ancestral home. But then he disliked Perkins, the Scotts' chauffeur, too. I wondered if it was because Perkins was hired by Uncle John, but decided it couldn't be, because Trixie was the Scotts' dependant, as well, and he liked Trixie.

He disliked the village schoolmaster, and when I asked him why, he said: 'He roars in church like the bull of Bashan. Drowns everyone with decent voices. Can't stand people who roar!'

Another if his dislikes was Andrew Pilks, the under-gardener.

'He wriggles like one of the worms he digs up,' explained Sebastian. 'He agrees with every blooming thing anyone suggests – especially Aunt June. He'll promise you anything, but in the end you'll find it's Dickson who delivers the goods. Can't stand people who wriggle!'

Chapter 4

We Celebrate

The holidays slipped away. We made the most of them, I can tell you. Every day we went out riding, or played tennis, or had a picnic. Sometimes we swam in the lake at home, but several times we rode to a lovely place called the Monks' Pool, near Bliss Castle, where you could dive off the rocks. Often we joined up with friends of the Scotts – the Eliots. They lived some miles away, on the other side of the river where the Monks' Pool was, and there were two of them – David, who was fifteen, and Patience, his half-sister. She was only eleven, but she was a jolly good swimmer. Sometimes they brought friends of their own, the Listers that Fiona had talked about when she'd been telling us about the tennis party, and a dark girl called Judy Milburne. We had a grand time!

Don't think I forgot about my dancing in all this. I practised faithfully every morning before breakfast, and often again before we went out. I didn't have to keep my practising secret, now that Aunt June had decided I was to be a dancing teacher, so I didn't lock the morning-room door when I worked in there.

Sometimes Caroline came and watched me, always asking me first if I minded her being there. Fiona came too – without asking – and there was a queer, scornful look on her face as she watched me doing *pliés*, *grands battements*, and *développés*. Once Sebastian came, but I think he considered it rather on the dull side – all those exercises, and no real dancing at all –

but he was too polite to say so. Or perhaps he realized that my *pliés* and *battements* were like his scales and exercises at the piano – dull, but necessary.

Well, as I say, the summer holidays passed like a flash, and one awful day we realized with a shock that it was the beginning of September, and school looming up in the all too near future. It was beginning to feel like autumn. Already the swallows were collecting on the eaves of the house and on the telegraph wires; the heather was covering the moors with a froth of purple, and the bracken was turning colour. Trixie and Aunt June were beginning to fuss about clothes – especially Fiona's, as she was going to her new school in Harrogate at the end of the month.

One marvellous thing happened to lighten the gloom. I received a slip of paper to say that, despite Miss Stanley's dismal forebodings, I had passed my School Certificate. I hadn't got my Matric with it, but I had achieved an ordinary, straightforward pass. I felt frightfully thrilled.

'We must have a real celebration,' Sebastian said when he heard the news. 'A triumphal picnic, what-ho!'

'What a fuss!' Fiona said disdainfully. 'Anyone would think Veronica had done something wonderful. Why, I passed that stupid exam last year, and I got umpteen "credits".'

'You're older than Veronica,' said Sebastian, quite ignoring the fact that there was only a month in it, and that Fiona *had* done jolly well to get her School Certificate at just under fifteen. 'And you didn't get Matric with it, anyway.'

'That was only because I didn't get a "credit" in French,' argued Fiona.

'So *you* say!' scoffed Sebastian. 'Anyhow, we're going to celebrate Veronica's triumph. You needn't come if you don't want to.'

'What sort of a celebration shall we have?' asked Caroline.

'A picnic.'

'We've had loads of picnics,' objected Fiona. 'We've had a picnic nearly every day.'

'Ah, but this is to be a different sort of picnic,' explained Sebastian. 'This is to be a picnic-by-night.'

'They would never let us,' said Caroline. 'They'd say it was dangerous. Why it should be more dangerous to have a picnic at night than during the day, I can't think – it isn't as if there were tramps, or wild animals—'

'I wish you'd shut up and let me finish what I was saying,' put in Sebastian. 'I was going to suggest we had our picnic by moonlight down by the lake. They couldn't object to that – not if we explained that it was a celebration. We could have a huge bonfire by the boathouse, and a swimming gala, and a concert—'

'Concert?' we echoed.

'Gramophone records,' stated Sebastian. 'That's a portable Aunt June has, isn't it?'

'Yes, but—'

'But me no buts! Surely she wouldn't object to us having the loan of it?'

'No, but—'

'Oh, all right, go on then – explain the "but",' laughed Sebastian.

'I was going to say I'm afraid most of the records are pretty well worn out,' I said apologetically. 'You see, I play them rather a lot. Still, there are *some* that are OK.'

'I've got lots,' pronounced Sebastian. 'Loads of 'em. I'll provide the records, if you get the loan of the gramophone.'

'Right-ho,' we agreed.

All that day we prepared for our celebration. We carted barrow-loads of wood, and armfuls of bracken and heather down to the lake, piled dead branches on top, until by sunset we had a goodly pile.

'It looks as if we were going to burn a witch, or do-in poor old Dido, Queen of Carthage!' laughed Sebastian. 'The funeral pyre, what-ho!'

'You do think of horrid things, Sebastian,' grumbled Caroline. 'Mind what you're doing with that gramophone! It's just where we'll fall over it in the dark. You'd better put it over here in the boathouse. We'll bring the records down tonight when we come. By the way, what about light?'

'The fire will light things up enough, but if you girls don't like undressing in the dark, you'd better bring along a couple of candles. It'll be pretty murky in this place, especially before the moon is up.'

By the way, you mustn't think that, while we were making all these preparations for a glorious blaze, we forgot about the food question. Far from it! Indeed it occupied a front place in our thoughts.

'What about sausages?' said Sebastian. 'I saw some going in as we came out this morning.'

'Going in where?'

'Into the jolly old Hall. If that green van we nearly collided with wasn't Joseph Brawn and Sons, Pork Butcher, Burneyhough, then my name's not Sebastian!'

'Gosh! I believe you're right!' exclaimed Caroline. 'What it is to go about noticing things!'

'I've noticed something else, too,' went on Sebastian. 'We didn't have those sausages for lunch today, and they certainly won't be for dinner – Aunt June is far above sausages for dinner! – and they won't be for your supper. Too indigestible, according to dear old Trixie, so—'

'So they'll still be there – in the larder!' I yelled.

'Jolly good detective work, my dear Watson!' laughed Sebastian. 'Well, how about scrounging some of them? They can't refuse when it's for a celebration.'

'By the way, Sebastian,' put in Caroline, 'how do we cook them?'

128

Sebastian considered.

'Well, there are two ways. Either in a civilized frying-pan over the fire, or skewered on sticks like savages.'

'Savages!' we yelled. Even Fiona thought that the sticks sounded more fun.

We crashed into the house and waylaid Trixie. She was very decent, and let us have quite a lot of sausages when she heard what we wanted them for – three each, to be exact. She also handed over a slab of fruit cake, and half a pound of chocolate biscuits.

'We can boil a kettle and have Kafékreme to drink,' said Caroline.

'With Fizzy-Fountain lemonade for the toasts,' added Sebastian. 'Must have toasts at a celebration!'

After we left Trixie we went down the drive to Sebastian's home to see what we could collect there. We got quite a lot of stuff. Some cheese straws that Bella had just made, half a chocolate cake, and four lamb chops.

'To be eaten cold, after we've finished the sausages,' pronounced Sebastian. 'Well, I think we're OK for food. Don't eat too much for supper, you lot! Spoil our feast.'

It was queer getting up from the supper table and, instead of going to bed as usual, trekking down to the lake laden with food and gramophone records. I'd brought some of Aunt June's, after all – the ones that weren't too bad. We met Sebastian down by the boathouse. He'd got there before us, and had spent his time poking handfuls of straw soaked with paraffin in between the branches all round the foot of the bonfire, so when we put a match to it, it broke into flames with a mighty roar and lit up the landscape all around. It looked quite like fairyland, with the reflection of the flames leaping and flickering in the water and making the trees round the edges of the lake look even more dark and mysterious than they did in the daytime. On our little beach it was as light as day, and though before we'd lit the fire we hadn't felt much like bathing, we now thought it would be great fun.

'Come on, let's get in!' yelled Sebastian. 'Did you bring the candles for the boathouse, you lot?'

I produced them and Sebastian lit them for us because we hadn't remembered to bring matches. After which the three of us retired to the boathouse and changed into our bathing costumes.

The candles made the boathouse seem quite mysterious – not a bit like its ordinary, everyday self. Even our ancient bathing costumes – the same ones that Sebastian had shown me on that never-to-be-forgotten morning so long ago – looked romantic.

'I'll have my usual stripy one,' I said. 'Rhapsody in Stripes by Molyneux.'

'What did you say?' demanded Fiona.

'Oh, nothing. It's only a joke between Sebastian and me,' I explained.

'Well, I must say it seems a terribly silly sort of joke,' declared Fiona. 'As if a famous person like Molyneux would have anything to do with an awful stripy costume like that!'

'That's the joke!' I said with a giggle, remembering the ridiculous things Sebastian had said about the other costumes.

Fiona just stared at me in disdain.

'Golly! I do wish I wasn't quite so fat!' Caroline said with a sigh. She'd put on Spotted Peril, and it certainly *was* on the small side for her. 'I wish I had a figure like you, Veronica. It's funny but I've only just noticed what a lovely figure you have. I wonder if it's all those dancing exercises you do?'

'No, of course not,' put in Fiona before I had time to answer. 'Anyway, Veronica's no slimmer than I am.'

'No,' admitted Caroline. 'But she's different, somehow. Veronica looks like – well, like a statue, if you see what I mean. You look more sort of floppy.'

'How dare you! I do not!' exclaimed Fiona in a temper. 'I'm *much* slimmer than she is.' Then she gave me a sidelong look, and added maliciously: 'I shouldn't wonder if Veronica got quite fat.'

Well, of course, I never took much notice of Fiona's remarks, but all the same a thrill of fear ran through me. Supposing – just supposing – Fiona were to be right and I did get fat. I looked down at myself anxiously, and saw in the candlelight with a feeling of relief that my thighs – the danger-spot with all dancers – were no bigger than they had been. Moreover the flesh on them, and on my calves when I felt them, was hard to the touch. Thank goodness I wasn't flabby!

'Come on, let's go!' said Caroline. 'It looks lovely out there. Sebastian's in already.'

We didn't stay in the water long, though. The bonfire made it look warm but actually it was pretty cold, and the wind, when you got out of the shelter of the boathouse, had a nip in it that told us autumn was on the way.

We dressed quickly and gathered round the fire. It had burnt down a lot while we were having our swim, but though it didn't look quite so spectacular now, it was beautifully hot, and warmed us up in no time. The kettle was singing, and the sausages were all ready skewered on the sticks, just waiting to be cooked.

'About our concert...' began Sebastian, sorting out the records. 'Let's have the heavier stuff now, shall we? Then we can put on the lighter things like Chopin's ballet music – *Les Sylphides* – when we've finished supper. What about giving an exhibition of some of *Les Sylphides*, Veronica? You know the ballet, surely?'

'Oh, yes – rather! Madame taught me the Waltz. It's the most lovely music to dance to.'

'Oh, *do* dance it for us,' pleaded Caroline.

'All right – I will, after supper,' I promised. 'Can't now – I'm too hungry.'

'We'll put the record over here by the milk,' Sebastian said. 'Then it won't get all mixed up with the others. What shall we have on now?'

'*Warsaw Concerto!*' I exclaimed, turning over the pile.

'Slushy!' pronounced Sebastian.

'Oh, I don't know,' I said. 'Personally I rather like it.'

'I think it's awful,' said Fiona.

'Let me see,' drawled Sebastian in his most infuriating manner, 'your taste in music, Fiona, is for what is commonly known as "Boogie-woogie", isn't it? Things like *I Gotta Have Love*. Then, after you've sung the touching words, you fill in by making queer noises like "cha-cha-cha", and "bom-bom-bom", and that's "Boogie-woogie"!'

'No, it isn't. You don't know anything about it.'

'Don't I? Well, the other day I heard a wench on the radio doing it, and I thought she was an escaped lunatic, but it turned out that she was a frightfully famous exponent of "Boogie-woogie"! so what?'

'If you don't stop talking rot and watch what you're doing, your sausages will be as black as a cinder.'

'Like 'em black as cinders,' said Sebastian, placidly inspecting his supper. 'They're not nearly black enough yet. Did anyone remember to bring the mustard?'

'*I* did!' I said triumphantly. 'The ready-bottled sort. Here it is. Gosh! No, it isn't. It's celery-salt. I must have mistaken the bottle.'

'You *would*!' pronounced Sebastian. 'You're no use for anything that hasn't something to do with dancing, Veronica! ... Kettle's boiling! Where's that Kafécreme, someone? Now *don't* say you've brought a tin of treacle or something instead!'

But all was well. Caroline found the tin of Kafécreme

nestling beside the lamb chops, and Sebastian measured it into a big jug with a tablespoon.

'Three cups each,' he said, holding the spoon poised in mid-air. 'Think that'll be enough?'

'I should say so – counting the three bottles of lemonade we've got for the toasts.'

We ate our meal to the uplifting strains of the London Symphony Orchestra playing the Rachmaninoff Concerto. It was one of Sebastian's records, and it was the one they played in the Coward film, *Brief Encounter*, that Sebastian and I had talked about that day I'd met him in the northbound train.

When we had finished the lamb chops, and the chocolate biscuits, and drunk the last drop of Kafécreme, Sebastian rinsed our mugs with lake water and refilled them with lemonade. Then he stood up.

'Ladies and gentlemen,' he announced. 'The King! You always toast the King first.'

We all rose to our feet and clinked glasses. Then Caroline said: Speech!'

'Well – er . . .' began Sebastian. 'On this august occasion of Veronica's passing her School Certificate, I would like to say that we all think – we think—'

'Go on! Go on!' we all yelled. 'What do we think?'

'That she's done jolly well to pass the thing at all,' went on Sebastian. 'It's a wonder to me that anyone ever passes it – considering the stupid things they ask!'

'But you've passed it yourself – ages ago,' said Caroline.

'I was meaning *ordinary* people,' stated Sebastian. 'I was never ordinary. Always the little genius, yours truly. I remember how fluently I used to prattle away in Latin when I was in my cradle. "*Nil desperandum*," I used to say. "*Veni, vidi, vici!*" "*Noblesse oblige.*"'

'But that last's French,' I objected.

'French or Latin – it was all the same to me,' said Sebastian loftily. 'Now what was I saying when I was so rudely inter- rupted? Oh, yes – I want to give you the toast of the evening – Miss Veronica Weston!'

They all stood up, but I sat still because you never stand up yourself when your health is being drunk.

'And now what about a spot of *Les Sylphides*, Veronica?' went on Sebastian. 'Can you manage to dance after all that supper?'

'I'll try!' I laughed.

Suddenly there was an exclamation from Fiona.

'Gosh! I've slipped! Somebody pushed me! Look what's happened!'

'Well, what *has* happened?' said Sebastian, not sounding very interested.

'I've sat on it!'

'Sat on what? Not the marmalade?'

'No, you idiot! On the record – the record of *Les Syl- phides*.'

There was a horrified silence. We all knew that Fiona had done it on purpose, but of course we couldn't prove it.

'You shouldn't have put it over there,' she said to Sebastian. 'How could I be expected to see it in the dark? I never expected a record to be there when I sat down.'

'I thought you said someone pushed you?'

'So they did.'

'Then in that case it wouldn't matter whether you could see it or not,' said Sebastian coldly. 'Well, that's the end of our dancing exhibition, Veronica. Never mind, we'll have it later on. And that's the end of the celebration, too – for *you*, Fiona, at any rate. You get out of here, and quick's the word!'

Fiona didn't argue – she knew Sebastian better than that! She left us without a backward glance. I have an idea she thought she'd got the best of it this time, as she'd had all the fun and we were left to clear up the mess. As Sebastian said, the beach wasn't big enough to hold both him and Fiona at that particular moment!

Chapter 5

A Pair of Ballet Shoes

Next morning I did my *barre* work as usual before breakfast. After that meal I went into the morning-room to finish off the centre work. I did a little piano practice as well, remembering Miss Martin's advice not to neglect my music, as it was very important that I should have a good musical groundwork if I wanted to be a dancer.

After I had finished it was nearly eleven o'clock. I changed out of my practice shoes and went off to the schoolroom, carrying them under my arm. Incidentally one of the ribbons was showing signs of wear and tear, so I resolved to sew it on before it got too bad to mend.

The others were all in the schoolroom when I got there: Caroline playing Patience on the hearthrug; Sebastian lounging by the french window; Fiona reclining on the ancient settee in one of the consciously graceful attitudes Sebastian hated so much. Her feet were tucked underneath her.

'I've got it out this time!' exclaimed Caroline, turning over the cards at lightning speed. 'No, I haven't! That king's in the way!'

'Put him in the space; then you *may* turn up a queen to go on top. Then the jack'll go on top of that, and you're out,' said Sebastian lazily.

'Gosh, so I am! What a brainwave! – if there *is* a queen. But there isn't, so I'm not out. Oh, dear! That's the fourth try this morning. I believe these cards have a spell on them!'

'How you can spend your time doing such silly things, I

can't imagine,' came Fiona's supercilious voice from the set-tee. 'Really, the things some people do!' She yawned deli-cately. 'For instance, those *pliés*, or whatever they're called, that Veronica does. Of all the stupid, ugly things—'

'I know they're not pretty,' I burst out. 'They're not meant to be. They're to keep your muscles supple. And *développés* are to give you strength—'

'Strength!' laughed Fiona. 'Are you aiming to be a strong man, then – like they have in a circus!'

I said nothing, knowing that it was quite useless to argue with Fiona when she was in a mood like this. Not so Sebas-tian, though. He liked nothing better than to take Fiona down a peg.

'I've seen you do some pretty silly-looking things,' he de-clared. 'For the uninitiated, I mean. What price those exercises you did when you learned to ride – lying down flat on Meli-sande's back and then sitting up again? Pretty mirth-provok-ing, what! Especially when she shied!'

'They were necessary!' snapped Fiona.

'So are Veronica's exercises. And they do at least make her graceful. You might try doing a few yourself, Fiona. They might improve your figure.'

Now Fiona's figure was perfect by any ordinary standards, and Sebastian knew it, but, as I say, he never could resist teasing her.

'How dare you!' she yelled, turning red. Then she uncurled her feet from beneath her, and stretched them out. As the settee back was between her and Sebastian, and Caroline was still busy with her Patience cards, neither of them saw any-thing peculiar about Fiona's feet. But I did! She was wearing a pair of pink satin ballet shoes – my shoes; the shoes Madame had given me; the shoes that had danced *Giselle* on Covent Garden stage. And this wasn't all either. She'd daubed a comic face on the toe of each of them with ink and red paint.

I gave a shriek of anguish. Then the blood rose to my head and I sprang at her. I'm afraid I lost my temper completely. I shook her as hard as I could, and then as she still laughed, I boxed her ears. Then I went on shaking until someone caught me by the arms and held me fast.

'What the dickens? Look here, this is going a bit too far!' said Sebastian's voice in my ear. 'Stop it, I say, Veronica! Fiona was only teasing.'

'Was she?' I yelled. 'Then what about my shoes?'

'Your shoes?' echoed Sebastian. Then he caught sight of Fiona's handiwork, and his voice froze.

'You did that, Fiona?'

'Yes, I did,' said Fiona. 'I think I've improved them, don't you? Brightened them up quite a bit. I never saw such mouldy-looking things when I took them in hand!'

'They were Madame's shoes!' I shouted at her. 'She'd danced *Giselle* in them. You *knew* how I loved them! You knew, Fiona. I told you!' Then I covered my face with my hands and burst into tears.

'You certainly have told us!' drawled Fiona. 'I'm sick to death of hearing about the stupid things! You ought to be grateful to me for ornamenting them a bit.' Then she added with a hateful little laugh: 'Cry-baby!'

But I was past being annoyed by a mere epithet. All I could think of was the awful thing that had happened to Madame's shoes. I just sobbed and sobbed, and Fiona went on laughing. Then, through my tears, I heard Sebastian say in a furious voice:

'You take that back, Fiona – what you said about Veronica!'

'I never take back what's true,' Fiona said sweetly. Then she turned and made a dash for the door. But Sebastian was there before her, barring her way.

'You go back and apologize to Veronica,' he ordered. 'On your knees, and be quick about it!'

'I will not! Let me go, this minute!'

Sebastian didn't move. Instead he said meaningly: 'Have you ever been beaten, Fiona?'

'Of course not! How dare you!' she said furiously. 'I'm a girl. Girls don't get beaten.'

'Don't they? Well, there's one who's going to, if you don't be quick with that apology,' drawled Sebastian. Then he snatched up one of my canvas practice shoes, that I'd put on the table, and stood brandishing it threateningly. 'Now, be quick! I can't stand here all day.'

At the time we were so het up that it all seemed terribly dramatic, but afterwards, when I thought about it, I saw how funny it really was – Sebastian standing there like an avenging angel, brandishing, instead of a flaming sword, an ancient canvas ballet shoe! Well, as I expect you know, an unblocked ballet shoe is as soft as a glove and couldn't possibly hurt anybody. So it says something for Sebastian's strength of personality that Fiona came back to where I stood, went down on her knees and made her apology. With a shock I realized that she was crying, a thing I'd never seen Fiona do before. I realized, too, that Sebastian had carried out his threat, and had effectively wiped off her face the self-satisfied look he so hated. Whether Fiona's tears were tears of shame, or anger, or both, I don't know.

'And now what about the shoes?' went on Sebastian, when she rose from her knees. 'What do you propose to do about them?'

'I d-don't know,' gulped Fiona.

'Well, start thinking about it, and be quick,' ordered Sebastian, still flourishing the shoe.

'I s-suppose the d-dry-cleaners...' hiccuped Fiona. 'M-mummy sent my party shoes to Britelites when I got ice-cream on them.'

'Good idea!' pronounced Sebastian. 'Get a letter written.

139

I'll dictate it.' He went to a cupboard, pulled out a writing pad, ink and a pen, and placed them on the table. 'Are you ready? . . .

'Messrs Britelite and Sons, Dyers and Cleaners,
Newcastle-upon-Tyne.

Dear Sir,
    Would you please dry-clean the ballet shoes I am sending you. I would be greatly obliged if you would take extra special care with them as they are irreplaceable and of great sentimental value. Thanking you in advance for the special care.

Yours faithfully,

(Miss) Fiona Scott'

Obediently Fiona wrote as he directed, and, glancing at Sebastian's face, I knew why!

'Now you'll have to find a box to pack them in,' he said inexorably when she'd finished. 'And lots of tissue paper. Oh, and some of that corrugated cardboard stuff to stop them getting squashed. And, of course, you'll have to pay for them yourself – out of your pocket money.'

'Well, can I go now?' Fiona asked when he had folded up the letter and put it into an envelope.

'Go?' Sebastian echoed. Then he struck an attitude. ' "Why get you gone! who is't that hinders you?" That's Shakespeare – *Midsummer Night's Dream* – in case you don't know. In other words, scram! Scoot! Begone! And the sooner the better!' His face had once more taken on its usual teasing aspect, and I knew that, as far as Sebastian was concerned, the episode was closed.

I often think how amazed grown-ups would be if they could know the things we do and think when they imagine we're 'playing nicely together' as they call it.

When Aunt June opened the schoolroom door not long after Fiona had fled, you'd have thought she'd have felt the tension in the air – the sobs, and slaps, the shrieks of anger and cold fury. But all she said, as she looked round, was: 'Ah! There you are – having a nice game of cards!' This was because she'd just caught sight of Caroline's Patience cards still lying on the hearthrug.

'Do you want us, Mummy?' Caroline asked hastily, trying to give me time to pull myself together.

'Well, yes, darling. I've just had a letter,' said Aunt June, holding up a sheet of thick, expensive notepaper. 'Such a nice letter. It's from dear Lady Blantosh of Blantosh Castle. She's having a garden fête – or if it's wet a "Do" in the parish hall – in aid of her Destitute Babies, and she wants us to help.'

'What at? Serving tea, or selling things?' demanded Caroline.

'Neither, dear. She wants you for the concert. I thought you might play the piano.'

There was a horrified silence. Then Caroline gave a positive wail of despair.

'Oh, *Mummy*! I couldn't – really, I couldn't! I'd die of fright – honestly I would. Fiona might do it though. She likes playing things in front of people.'

'U – m,' Aunt June said doubtfully. 'Fiona isn't as good as you are, Caroline. By the way, where *is* Fiona?'

'She – er – she went out,' stammered Caroline.

'Well, you might ask her about it,' Aunt June persisted. 'I do think you might at least *try* to play something, Caroline. Nobody will mind, I'm sure, if you make a few mistakes. What on earth is the use of your father giving you expensive music lessons if you never play anything to anybody?'

Poor Caroline grew red.

'I'm sorry, Mummy,' she said miserably. 'I just can't help it.'

'Well, you'll really have to do *something*,' went on Aunt June inexorably. 'Lady Blantosh says she's counting on you.'

Suddenly Caroline gave such a whoop that poor Aunt June jumped visibly.

'*I* know! Veronica will dance. She knows lots of dances don't you, Veronica? There's that one about a Sugar Plum Fairy that you were telling us about at the celebration, and that other one – Les something or other ... Veronica knows lots of them, Mummy!'

Aunt June turned to stare at me, and I was thankful that by this time my tears had dried.

'Dance?' she repeated, as if she'd never heard of the word. 'You don't mean that atrocious tap dancing, I hope?'

'Oh *no*, Aunt June!' I exclaimed. 'Caroline means ballet. The dances she's talking about are out of ballets – the Dance of the Sugar Plum Fairy is out of the *Casse Noisette*, and the Waltz is out of *Les Sylphides*. Then I expect she's seen me practising the Odette solo out of *Swan Lake* ...'

I stopped abruptly, afraid lest Aunt June might think I was wasting my time practising the dances from the ballets, but to my surprise she only said: 'Well, that's certainly an idea, if we can't think of anything better. I'll ask Lady Blantosh what she thinks about it. She's got some famous person, Madame somebody or other – I think she's a singer – coming up from London especially to open the fête. Under the circumstances she mightn't think dancing quite – quite – well, you know what I mean – not high class enough.'

'Ballet is one of the arts,' said Sebastian's voice from the window. 'You couldn't get anything higher class than ballet.'

We all turned to stare at Sebastian. I think we'd forgotten that he was still there.

'Indeed,' Aunt June said coldly, and I knew by the sound of her voice that she didn't like Sebastian any more than he liked her. 'And what do you know about it, may I ask?'

'Oh, I know something about ballet,' Sebastian confessed casually. 'I've often been to Covent Garden with my father.'

'I see,' said Aunt June, not sounding as if she were really very interested. 'Well, as I say, I shall consult Lady Blantosh. If she wants you to dance, Veronica, I suppose she'll provide you with something suitable to wear?'

'Oh, but I've got a frock, Aunt June!' I exclaimed eagerly, thinking of the snowy *tutu* hanging in my part of Fiona's wardrobe. 'And if I need anything else, Miss Martin will lend it me – I know she will. She often lends her students costumes for shows.'

Aunt June went out, muttering things about her family and its shortcomings, and we were left to discuss the concert. I wasn't terribly excited. According to Caroline and Fiona, Lady Blantosh wasn't a very exciting person, though there was no denying the fact that she had a heart of gold. Still, I didn't feel that she would appreciate the lovely Waltz from *Les Sylphides*. All of which goes to show how Fate has things up her sleeve for you, because that self-same concert proved to be the turning-point of my life.

Chapter 6

Les Sylphides

The next morning Aunt June said that she had rung up Blantosh Castle, and Lady Blantosh wanted me to dance at her garden fête.

'She seemed quite keen about it,' said Aunt June. 'I was really most surprised. And now I suppose you'll have to see about your costume, Veronica. You think Miss Martin would lend you one?'

'I'm quite sure she would,' I answered. 'Couldn't I go into town this afternoon? Trixie told me yesterday that she had some shopping to do, so I could go with her. I shall need a gramophone record of the Waltz besides the frock.'

'I thought you had the record,' Aunt June said. 'I understood Caroline to say you'd been using it to practise with?'

'I – as a matter of fact it's pretty well worn out,' I stammered.

'I never imagined gramophone records wore out,' stated Aunt June. 'I always thought they went on for ever.'

'It's not worn out,' came Caroline's voice. 'At least it is, but it's squashed as well.'

'Whatever do you mean?'

'I mean Fiona sat on it,' said Caroline. 'She did it on purpose, too!'

'Oh, no,' said Aunt June, who always took Fiona's part. 'If Fiona sat on it, I'm sure it was an accident. But, in any case, if the record is broken, of course you must get another one, Veronica.'

'I'll pay for it myself,' I volunteered. To tell you the truth, my conscience was pricking me a little when I remembered that I had worn out Aunt June's record by dancing to it, not by listening to it to improve my music as she thought, even if Fiona *had* sat on it afterwards.

But Aunt June said no; she'd pay for it herself as the garden fête was her affair, and what about the other dances?

'You did say you could do two?' she added.

'I'd simply love to,' I answered, 'if you think the people won't be bored.'

Aunt June said that that was beside the point – everyone went to a garden fête prepared to be bored. Anyhow, Lady Blantosh had mentioned two dances – one before the interval and the other after.

'She did say that you ought to have a third ready – in case of an encore,' added Aunt June. 'But I shouldn't think that's very likely!'

'Then I'll do the *Swan Lake* solo,' I said, 'and the Waltz from *Les Sylphides*. Then if they *do* want another, I can do the Dance of the Sugar Plum Fairy – I've got the record for that.'

'Then you'll need two new ones,' said Aunt June.

'Yes, the Tchaikovsky *Swan Lake* solo and the Chopin *Les Sylphides*,' I answered. 'Goodness! I hope there *is* a recording of the *Swan Lake* solo; I've never seen one. Anyway, I'll ask at the shop.'

I left Trixie in the town doing the shopping while I went to see Miss Martin. She was most interested when she heard about the garden fête, and she lent me a lovely white *Sylphides* dress. She packed it into a cardboard box, saying that of course I should have to iron it out before I wore it. For the benefit of those who don't know, I must explain what a *Sylphides* dress is like. It has a tight-fitting bodice made of satin

– dull, if possible – and a long, full net skirt reaching to the middle of the calves. It has tiny cape-like sleeves, and little wings fastened on to the back of the bodice.

Miss Martin also lent me some pale pink tights, which she said I'd need if I was going to wear a classical *tutu*. They weren't real silk, because these are almost impossible to get nowadays, but they were made of very fine lisle-thread, and they were fully fashioned. I can tell you they stayed up an awful lot better than the artificial silk ones I already had! Miss Martin also happened to have a pair of pink satin blocked shoes, exactly the right size – fourteen – so I bought them for twelve and six out of my own money.

After this, I took a bus back to the centre of the town, where the gramophone shops were. And here my good luck changed to bad. Each shop I went to had every waltz of Chopin's except the one I wanted! They hadn't a recording of the Odette solo out of *Le Lac des Cygnes* either. The salesman in the last shop I went to was most obliging. He brought out all the catalogues and we pored over them together. Finally he stood upright, shook his head, and said that he was *afraid* there wasn't a recording of that solo, of if there was, he certainly hadn't come across it.

'Well, have you the Waltz from *Les Sylphides* – Chopin?' I asked despairingly.

The man said he thought he had. If I would wait just a moment . . . He retired to the back of the shop, and began to run his hands over the hundreds of records that were stacked on the shelves, whilst I waited at the counter in a frenzy of impatience. Finally, he came back and said he was frightfully sorry, but that the gentleman who was in this morning must have bought the last one.

I could have wept with disappointment. I could also cheerfully have killed the gentleman who'd come in that morning and taken away my beloved Waltz!

'Can we order it for you?' asked the record man, politely. But I explained that it was no use – it wouldn't be in time, because the thing I wanted it for was on Saturday.

All the way home in the car I wondered what I should do about it; whether I should cry off the whole thing, which I knew would make Aunt June furious; or whether I should just dance the Sugar Plum Fairy and trust to luck that the record behaved itself, and didn't go on playing the same bit over and over in that maddening way records have when they're getting old. The only other alternative was to ask someone at the garden fête to play for me, but to be quite frank, I didn't think it at all likely that anyone could play Chopin's music, let alone Tchaikovsky's, at a moment's notice – even if anyone *had* the music for the Odette solo.

I was so silent that Trixie asked if I felt ill.

'No – not ill. Just worried,' I told her.

Then, just as we approached the Hall gates, I had a sudden idea . . . Sebastian! I wondered if, by any chance, he had any of the records I needed. I was amazed I hadn't thought of it before.

'Trixie!' I shrieked. 'I must get out quickly! Perkins – stop!'

Perkins obligingly stopped and I got out.

'It's all right – I'll walk up,' I said. 'You needn't wait. I'm going to see Sebastian. I've just had a brainwave.'

The casement windows of the lodge were open and, as I walked over the grass towards the little green door, the sound of music reached me. Someone was playing Grieg's *Holberg Suite*, and playing it extremely well.

I stood still and listened. I had often tried to play it myself, but had never been able to render it with such – 'authority' I think is the word. The music began on a rising crescendo of lovely, broken chords; then came the haunting melody, picked out by the left hand. After this, the loud bass part, and a new air brought in by more broken chords in the treble.

Then I knew that the unseen pianist was none other than Sebastian – Sebastian whom I had never heard play, but whose secret ambition I knew was to make music his career. Yes, I knew without a doubt that it was Sebastian. It was *like* Sebastian. Nobody but he could play it in exactly that way.

The music ended on the final, crashing chords, and the trill. There was a pause. Then, before I had recovered from my daydream, another melody came floating out of the window – a dreamy melody, this time; a melody that made you think of green woods, and graceful larch boughs of glimmering water and the pale evening sky ... the Waltz from *Les Sylphides* ...

Before I knew what I was doing, I had kicked off my heavy shoes, thrown aside my cardigan, and was dancing. There, in my faded cotton frock, my feet bare, on the strip of velvet lawn which was my first stage, I danced the Waltz as I had never danced it before. The lacy, arching trees, the emerald turf, the pale ghost of a new moon between the larch boughs – I put them all into my dancing. It wasn't till afterwards, when I thought it over, that I realized I had danced the Waltz in its rightful setting – a woodland glade.

Then suddenly the dance was ended. The music died away, and I was brought down to earth by a voice from the window – Sebastian's voice. It said: 'Very nice, Veronica! I watched you all through. It was grand!'

An awful feeling of disappointment shot through me.

'Oh – but I thought it was *you* playing, Sebastian.'

He laughed.

'Oh, no! That was the jolly old gramophone – Eileen Joyce, in fact. I bought that record in town this morning, so I was trying it to see what it was like. Then I looked out of the window and saw you dancing.'

'It's queer,' I said, 'but when I was listening to the *Holberg*

Suite, I thought how like *you* it was, Sebastian. That's strange, isn't it?'

'The *Holberg Suite*?' repeated Sebastian. 'You heard that too? Oh, the record I was talking about – the Eileen Joyce – was that last thing, the Chopin waltz. It was *me* playing the Grieg *Holberg Suite* on the piano all right. I often play it – it appeals to me.'

I gave a sigh of relief.

'Oh, I'm so glad! I'd have been terribly disappointed if the *Holberg Suite* hadn't been you, Sebastian.'

'What made you come down here, anyway?' asked Sebastian, swinging himself over the window-sill to stand beside me on the garden path. 'Were you just passing, or what?'

'Oh, no. I've just come back from Newcastle,' I explained. 'I went in with Trixie to borrow a frock to wear at the garden fête on Saturday and to try to get a record for my dance. But they hadn't got it – a beastly man had been in this morning, and pinched the last one – so I was coming to see if *you* had it . . .' Then I gave a shriek of joy. 'But of course everything's all right now – you *have* got it. I can borrow yours.'

'Welcome!' said Sebastian promptly. 'If you wouldn't mind telling me which record you're talking about.'

'I mean the one I just heard, of course – the one I danced to – the Waltz from *Les Sylphides* – the one—'

'The beastly gentleman pinched,' laughed Sebastian. 'That would be me all right! I got it this morning at Windows. You can have it and welcome. As a matter of fact I was going to hand it over to you – to make up for the one Fiona squashed.'

'Oh, *thank* you, Sebastian,' I said. 'That was most awfully decent of you. Well, now there's only the *Swan Lake* Odette solo. I suppose you haven't a record of *that*?'

He shook his head.

'I doubt if there is one. I can play it, though.'

I stared at him unbelievingly.

'Not really?'

'Honest injun.'

He swung himself back into the room again, sat down at the piano, remained for a moment in thought, then played my solo – perfectly, and with that same indefinable air of authority I had noticed in the *Holberg Suite*.

'And you'll play it for me at the garden fête?' I said when he'd finished.

He made a face.

'I'll do it for you, Veronica,' he said, 'because you're in a jam. We *artistes* must stick together. Otherwise I wouldn't go near the dashed thing!'

'Oh, Sebastian – you *are* decent!' I said again. 'I'll never, never forget it. I'll be grateful always.'

'Utter not rash vows, fair lady!' said Sebastian, relapsing once more into his usual bantering self. 'You don't know what I might want you to do for me in the near future, when you're a world-famous *ballerina* and I'm a poor, struggling musician, playing at street corners to earn my daily crust!'

'I think,' I said looking back at him, 'it's much more likely that *you'll* be a world-famous conductor, and I'll be a struggling dancer, trying to eke out a living on the halls!'

'Well, here's the record,' said Sebastian, handing it over to me. 'And now, get thee hence, damsel! I have work to do!' So saying, he shut the window firmly, and in a moment or two I heard the sound of scales being played on the piano. There being nothing else for it, I went up the path towards the house, holding the precious record carefully under my arm.

Chapter 7

I Meet an Old Friend

It was wet on Saturday, so the garden fête was hastily changed into a Bring and Buy Sale, and was to be held in the parish hall instead of in the grounds of Blantosh Castle. There was one good thing about it – I'd have a proper stage to dance on, instead of just grass. Grass might have done all right for the Waltz, but it certainly would have been awkward for the other things, as I couldn't have done them *en pointe*.

Of course we *would* have a puncture! It was the little car too because something had gone wrong with the big one, and you had to get out and fix a jack under the wheel. Perkins wasn't with us, either, because Aunt June said there wasn't room for him. She was right too. By the time Fiona had spread herself out so that her frock wouldn't get crushed, and Caroline had got in front with a whole lot of cakes that Aunt June was taking over for the tea, there wasn't any too much room for me and my precious *tutu*. I'd packed the *Sylphides* dress in a suitcase along with my tights, shoes, and other things, and put them in the boot.

'I do wish you wouldn't squash me, Veronica!' Fiona said, as we drove off. 'I've never known anything take up so much room as that frock.' She shot a venomous glance at my un-offending ballet dress. 'Couldn't you have put it in the boot as well?'

'It would have got frightfully crushed,' I retorted. 'Really, the only way to carry a *tutu* is out flat like this.' I glanced down with pride at the snowy ring of tarlatan, resting lightly on my knees.

'Well, it wouldn't really matter if it *was* crushed,' went on Fiona. 'A village concert like this isn't at all an important thing, you know.'

'Every time you perform is important when you're a dancer,' I told her. 'You must always do your best, no matter who your audience is.'

'But you're *not* a dancer,' insisted Fiona. 'You're only going to *teach* dancing, so I don't see that it matters.'

I blushed hotly, having totally forgotten my guilty secret. Then just at this moment, as I say, we got a puncture. In a way it was a relief, because it stopped me having to answer Fiona's awkward questions, but in another it was awful. Aunt June didn't seem to know the least thing about punctures. At first she wanted Caroline and me to walk back home – about a mile and a half – and bring Perkins to change the wheel, but, as I pointed out, by the time we'd got there and Perkins had walked back with us to the car – because he'd *have* to walk seeing that there wasn't another car – the Bring and Buy would be over.

In the end, Caroline and I did it, whilst Fiona made what she considered to be helpful suggestions, being very careful all the time not to touch anything that might dirty her hands. Fortunately I'd often seen Daddy's friend, Mr Salmon, take off a wheel, and sometimes I'd helped him, so I knew all the things you had to do and not to do – like not jacking up the car until you'd got the nuts unscrewed, and putting two chocks of wood under the back wheel to stop the car slipping off the jack, once you'd got it wound up, and so on. Still, it's one thing to watch a grown-up person do a thing, and even to help him, and quite another to do it all by yourself. However, as I say, we managed it at last; we even remembered to put the tools away.

We got back into the car, and Aunt June told Fiona to hold my frock, because my hands were anything but clean. I have an idea she was thinking more of the effect my muddy *tutu* would have on Lady Blantosh than my own feelings in the matter!

By the time we got to the parish hall and had parked the car, the Bring and Buy was well under way. We went into the building by a back entrance in order to avoid the masses of people who were surging about in the main hall. When we got to the ladies' cloakroom we had to wash, owing to the puncture, and I can tell you it took us ages to get clean because we'd managed to get an awful lot of oil on ourselves, as well as mud, and oil is about the worst thing on earth to wash off! We used the same water to save time, and bumped our heads together during the process. As the saying goes – 'More haste, less speed!' It was certainly so in our case!

At last we were clean once more, and then I began to dress in readiness for my first dance, while Fiona washed her hands in hot water in preparation for her pianoforte solo. It was to be one of Brahms' waltzes, and I must say, when I'd heard her playing it yesterday, she didn't do it awfully well. She kept the loud pedal down all the time to cover up her mistakes, and her fingering was all wrong, because she never could be bothered to practise slowly. Fiona always tackled a new piece of music at top speed, and then said she 'knew it'.

Caroline had propitiated Aunt June by agreeing to play a duet with Fiona, on condition that she played the bottom part, because no one ever listened to that.

Meanwhile I had retired behind a screen that someone had thoughtfully provided, and removed all my things – that's the worst of a ballet dress; you can't leave anything on underneath or it shows. I pulled on my tights, wriggled my jock-belt on top to keep them up – and me in! – and then, with the utmost care, I proceeded to insert myself into the *tutu*. It's made all in one with the frilly trunks, so you step into it, feet first. Fortunately it had a zip fastener down the side, so I didn't have an awful lot of hooks and eyes to do up. Finally, I put on my beautiful pink satin point shoes, criss-crossing the ribbons, the outside ribbon over the inside one, and tying them in a neat little bow at the side of the ankle. I sleeked back my hair in the severely classical style, put a net over it, and fastened it down firmly at the sides and the back with hairgrips, so that it would not come down, no matter how many *pirouettes* I did. After which I made up my face – not with heavy greasepaint, for there was no artificial lighting to speak of in the parish hall, but with ordinary lipstick, eyeshadow, and powder. I'd bought them all in Newcastle yesterday. I'd also bought an eyebrow-pencil and I used it to lengthen my eyes a little at the corners. When I stepped back to see the effect in the long glass, thoughtfully provided by the same unknown person, I gasped. Was it really me – that slim dancer, clad in the traditional, classic *tutu*; that girl with the dreamy face, and large, dark eyes? Did those beautifully shaped limbs – slender, yet rounded – really belong to me? For a few seconds I stood quite still, refusing to believe it. Then, with a singing in my heart, I knew that it was true!

'Veronica!' came Caroline's voice, shattering my daydream. 'Veronica! Are you nearly ready? They're just going to begin the concert now. Lady Blantosh is taking her Madame Some-body on to the platform to make a speech. Then, after she's finished, it's Fiona's Brahms, and after that it's your dance.'

I came out from behind the screen, and there was a queer little silence that I knew was admiration. Then Caroline looked round – she'd been watching the people on the platform through a crack in the door.

'Veronica! How perfectly *gorgeous* you look!'

'Thank you,' I said, dropping a curtsy. 'It *is* a nice frock, isn't it?'

'Oh, but it isn't just the frock,' persisted Caroline. 'It's *you*, Veronica. You look like a flower, doesn't she, Fiona?'

Fiona said nothing, but I knew by her silence, and by the way she turned her back on me, that I looked nice. I'm afraid that I gloried in it!

Then, as I stood there, a startling thing happened. A voice came from the hall beyond our little dressing-room – a voice whose tones I knew well. How often had I hung upon them in those far-off days in London! I couldn't believe my ears, because the voice, speaking in broken English, was Madame's voice!

I dashed to the door in an effort to see the stage.

'Look out!' came Caroline's warning tones. 'They'll see you! It'll spoil the whole thing if they see you.'

'But don't you *understand*,' I said, shaking her off. 'It's Madame – Madame herself!'

'It's Madame Viret,' Fiona said stiffly.

'Of course I know it's Madame!' I exclaimed. 'I don't need you to tell me that. No one else – no one in all the world could speak just like that. It's Madame – my Madame! She taught me how to dance.'

Fiona stared at me.

'Oh, no – she couldn't have. She couldn't *possibly* have taught you to dance, Veronica. You're making a mistake; lots of people talk in broken English. She's a very famous person; besides, she's a singer. Mummy said so.'

'Then Aunt June's wrong,' I said flatly. 'She isn't a singer at all – she's a dancer. I mean, she *was* a dancer, and of course she's famous – I told you so, only you wouldn't believe me. She was the most famous dancer of her day, but of course you can't go on dancing for ever and ever, so now she's passing on her art to other people.'

'You needn't get so excited about it,' Fiona said loftily.

'But I *am* excited! I'm – I'm – oh, just to think of dear

155

Madame out there in the hall, only a few steps away, where I can see her, and speak to her—'

'Well, you certainly can't go rushing out dressed like that,' Fiona told me. 'You'll just have to wait until the performance is over.'

I sighed. Of course she was right. I certainly couldn't dash out into the middle of all those people, dressed like a swan in *Le Lac des Cygnes*! Much less could I throw my arms round Madame's neck, and cry for joy, as I dearly wanted to. As Fiona said, I should just have to wait. And wait I did, shivering a little with nerves and excitement.

Then it was time for my solo. Sebastian came to the door of the dressing-room to see if I was ready – a strange, tidy, grown-up Sebastian, with his usually ruffled black hair sleeked down flat, and long black trousers, instead of the familiar well-worn riding-breeches or khaki shorts.

'Are you coming, Veronica?'

He sat down at the grand piano and waited, whilst I walked on to the stage in the way Madame had taught me, and stood there at the back, hands crossed on my snowy *tutu*.

And then the well-known music filled the room. Sebastian played by memory, so he was able to watch me all the time. He was the most perfect accompanist, seeming to know by instinct exactly when to slow the music up just a little, and when to quicken it so that I didn't have to hold my positions too long. No wonder I danced as I had never danced before. I danced principally for Madame, to show her that I hadn't forgotten all the things she'd taught me, but I danced for Sebastian too – Sebastian playing for me so beautifully that his music made me feel as if I were floating on the melody, like a real swan on a moonlit lake.

I had forgotten all about the people in the hall, and when the dance ended and they burst into applause, I was terribly surprised and taken aback. I curtsied low as Madame had taught me – first this way, then that; then ran off into the wings (which consisted of a couple of large screens) to recover my self-possession.

The clapping went on and on. In fact it got louder, if anything.

'You'll have to do something else, Veronica,' said Sebastian's voice in my ear. 'What about the Sugar Plum Fairy? That's the right dress for it, isn't it?'

'Oh, yes,' I panted. 'Do you think I might have a minute's rest?'

'Of course,' said Sebastian. 'Tell you what – I'll go back and play them something for a couple of seconds. That'll keep them quiet!'

I leaned against the wall and relaxed, listening to Sebastian playing the *Holberg Suite*. The audience seemed to like it tremendously, for they clapped like anything when he finished, and if Aunt June hadn't appeared on the stage with the record of the Sugar Plum Fairy, and announced that her niece, Veronica Weston, would dance again, I think that Sebastian would have had to give an encore. Aunt June didn't look too pleased, I imagined. Sebastian *had* rather shown up Fiona's bad playing, but of course it wasn't his fault – he'd merely been giving me time to get my breath.

I walked out into the wings, and rose *sur les pointes*. The first notes of Tchaikovsky's music were falling on the air like drops of ice tinkling into a crystal goblet. I saw in my imagination the snowy woods round Bracken Hall on a winter's day – the fir trees standing motionless, like enchanted princesses, their frosted arms outspread. I heard in my mind the church bells sounding thin and unreal in the cold, blue air. All this I thought of as I executed the crisp, clear-cut steps of that wonderful dance of the Sugar Plum Fairy. I was a maiden of the ice; a snow queen; a frosted fairy of pink and silver,

157

I was a maiden of the ice, a snow queen

with a brittle crown of frozen dewdrops on my head. All this I tried to express in my dancing.

The clapping burst out louder than ever when I finished the dance. I had to come back on to the stage three times and curtsy, and even then it didn't stop. Some people at the back began to stamp their feet and shout *encore*, and finally I had to explain that I really couldn't dance any more just now because I hadn't got any breath left, but that I would dance again after the interval. Then I ran off into the dressing-room, and flopped into a chair, breathing hard. The Dance of the Sugar Plum Fairy isn't at all an easy dance to do, though it looks so charming and effortless.

'Oh, Veronica – you were wonderful!' Caroline said. 'I never imagined you could dance like that. I never imagined *anyone* could. I want to learn to do it. I want to learn *now*! Do you think Mummy would let me leave Miss Gilchrist and go to your Miss Martin?'

'I expect she would – if you asked her,' I laughed. 'Miss Martin's a lot cheaper!'

'Well, I'm going to ask her. And by the way,' added Caroline looking round, 'where's Fiona? It's our duet after this.'

'It's all right – I'm here,' came Fiona's voice from the window. 'You needn't get all hot and bothered.'

'But I *am* hot and bothered. I'm simply terrified!'

'Don't be silly!' snapped Fiona crossly. 'What do a few stupid people matter, anyway? They don't know a thing about music or – or dancing – or anything. They'd clap you no matter how ghastly you were – even if you played wrong notes all the time. They always do at these things!'

I glanced at Fiona curiously. I had an idea she didn't like the way the people had applauded my dance.

I had plenty of time to change, as my other dance wasn't until after the interval. I could hear poor Caroline's bass notes booming away, as she and Fiona played their duet. As I carefully hung up the *tutu* on a peg, and slipped on the long white frock Miss Martin had lent me, I heard Fiona galloping away in the treble, with the loud pedal down all the time as usual. She was playing as if she were in a rare temper, I thought.

I released my hair from the net for the *Sylphides* dance, letting it fall naturally on my shoulders, only fastening it at the sides with a couple of hairgrips, so that it shouldn't get in my way. Almost before I knew it, I was back on the stage again, dancing to Sebastian's gramophone. Sebastian himself was crouched down beside it, and I knew instinctively that he would stop it at exactly the right moment.

I can't say that I danced the Waltz as well as I had danced it that day on the grass outside Sebastian's window, but I think I did it fairly well. As Fiona said, the people were easily pleased, and they clapped as much as they had done for the other dances – indeed, I think more. When at last I escaped into the dressing-room, Fiona was looking like a veritable thundercloud.

'They like you a lot better than our duet, Veronica,' sighed Caroline. 'And no wonder! I think our duet was *awful*. I lost my place twice, and Fiona—'

'You needn't say *I* lost my place!' yelled Fiona. 'I wouldn't do anything so silly!'

'No, but you played half of it in sharps instead of flats,' said Caroline bluntly.

'I did not!'

'Yes, you did!'

And then, before there was a stand-up fight between the two of them, the dressing-room door opened, and someone came in – a small, graceful person beautifully dressed in black. She wore a tiny black hat, trimmed with white feather flowers and a veil, long white gloves, and little button-up boots of French kid.

'*Madame!*' I shrieked. Then, forgetting all about Fiona and her supercilious stare, forgetting all about the other girls in the room, forgetting everything, I threw my arms round Madame's neck, and burst into tears.

'My leetle one! *Mon petit chou*,' said Madame, patting me gently. 'So much improved! By zat I mean ze dancing and ze ap-pearance. Ze technique – he has advanced, yes. But zat will improve still more. You have had many lessons, *chérie*?'

'Oh, yes – I've had quite a lot of lessons from the Miss Martin you told me about,' I said, drying my eyes. 'But, of course, not as many as I'd have had if I'd been able to stay in London.'

'Ah, well – per'aps zat ees all for ze best. Who knows?' pronounced Madame surprisingly.

'But how could it possibly be for the best?' I asked. 'What do you mean?'

'I mean…' Madame considered the matter gravely. 'I mean eef you stay in London, you dance. Eef you are gone in Northumberland, you *think* – and you dance a leetle also. But ze *think* – he is important, yes! Your thoughts, zey are charming ones – all about ze woods, and ze 'ills, and ze flowers of zis so-beautiful Northumberland. I see eet in your dancing.'

'Then you really think I've improved, Madame?' I asked eagerly.

'*Sans doute*. You 'ave improve incomparably,' answered Madame, who loved to use long words, though she *did* accent them all wrongly. 'And your ap-pearance, *chérie*, your looks, zay are *tout à fait ravissantes*! Ze country air, and ze good food – zey 'ave assuredly transformed my leetle ugly duckling into a leetle swan – yes! Ze arms so round' – Madame put several r's into the word – 'ze shoulders – ah, *beau-ti-ful*!'

'You don't think I've got *fat*, Madame?' I said in horror, remembering Fiona's words at the celebration.

Madame laughed like a tinkle of little silver bells.

'*Oh, là! là!* Fat? But no, no, *no*! You are quite ze perfect figure for ze *danseuse*. So slender – so rounded! And ze deemples, zey 'ave come, so and *so*!' She pressed her white-gloved finger gently into my cheeks. '*Oh, là! là!* And to find you here?'

'I think it's me who ought to say that!' I laughed. 'After all I *live* here now, you know. But you, Madame – to find *you* at a – a—'

'To find me at a Bring What You Buy – zat amuse you, hey? Well, it amuse me, too! But to do the obligation for my dear Lady Blantosh, I do things strange to me!' she laughed. 'Eet ees so al-ways! She command; I obey! Eet ees right, yes?'

'Sebastian says everybody does what Lady Blantosh wants!' I laughed. 'He says she's got the evil eye!'

'Ze evil eye?' echoed Madame. 'But 'ow ees eet? Ah, I ondairstand – ze squint! But no, I think eet ees ze eye full of good, even eef eet does not look quite straight.'

That was just like Madame, I thought – always to think the best of people. Incidentally it wasn't the least bit like Sebastian. He didn't like Lady Blantosh because she squinted and wore awful clothes, and nothing would make him see how good and kind she really was.

Suddenly I looked round the dressing-room. Fiona had disappeared long since – I think she didn't like Madame's flowery way of speaking, and her lavish compliments. Caroline and the other girls had gone too, and we were alone.

'Madame!' I said urgently.

'Well, my leetle one?'

'Madame – I want to dance!' I burst out. 'I *must* dance!'

'*Mais oui!* But of *course* you must dance! Of course! Of course! What else?'

'It's no use saying "of course" like that,' I went on. 'You see Aunt June doesn't realize it – or Uncle John. No one does but me – and Sebastian.'

'Sebastian?' repeated Madame.

'He's the boy who played for me.'

'Ah yes, the pianist?' said Madame. 'A very talented young man, that one! He has the touch quite exquisite! He will go far!'

'Yes, but what about me?' I said. 'What about my dancing, Madame?' I knew that soon, soon people would come and snatch Madame away, and I'd see her no more. 'What must I do?'

'You must dance, *naturellement*,' Madame said definitely, gesticulating with her small, exquisite hands. 'I will speak to ze good aunt – and ze *oncle* too, eef eet ees *nécessaire*. I weel arrange! Leave eet to me.'

'Oh, Madame – *thank* you!' I said fervently. I had implicit faith in Madame when she wore her determined look as she did now. 'I *will* leave it all to you.'

'Then *au revoir*, my leetle one! I see you soon – in London!' With a final pat on my cheek she was gone, and I was left in the dressing-room alone.

For a long time I stood quite still in the middle of the empty room, while thoughts crowded upon me. For the first time I saw Madame as she really was. In London I had merely taken her for granted as the greatest dancer of her time, but now I realized that she wasn't young any more. Her dark hair was already streaked with grey, and her figure was no longer that of the girl I had so passionately adored in the photograph on her studio wall. But I knew, also, that she would never really grow old; that she would always remain beautiful be-cause of her charm and her vivacity; because of the grace of her every movement, her exquisite hands that spoke to you more eloquently than words, but above all because of the kindness and generosity that looked out of her large, dark eyes. Madame was one of those women about whom people say: 'Amazing how she keeps her youth! Why, let me see, she must be – well, old enough to be a grandmother!'

I thought of all this as I stood there, and lots of other things besides – Jonathan, and Mrs Crapper (I hadn't thought of them for a long time – I confess it!) – and above all, the Sadler's Wells Ballet School. It seemed a lot nearer now!

Madame was as good as her word. Going home in the car Aunt June broached the subject.

'That Madame Viret – I forget the rest of her outlandish name – was quite impressed with your dancing, Veronica,' she said as we left the parish hall behind. 'She thinks you ought to take it up professionally.'

She paused, and I waited breathlessly.

'A school called Sadler's Wells I understood her to say is the best place to learn. It's in London,' went on Aunt June. 'She thinks you ought to go there. In fact she is arranging for an interview – or whatever it is they call it.'

'Audition,' I said.

'Yes – audition. She thinks that, under the circumstances, they might give you a scholarship.'

'Oh, Aunt June!'

'It isn't a boarding school,' continued Aunt June. 'We'd have to arrange for somewhere for you to stay during the term – of course you would come back here in the holidays. Perhaps that Mrs Cripps—'

'Crapper,' I corrected gently but firmly.

'Crapper, then. She seems a good-hearted sort of woman. Perhaps we could persuade her to have you as a paying guest.'

'I'm sure she'd have me,' I assured Aunt June.

'Well, yes – I think you must really go,' said Aunt June just as if it was her idea in the first place, and she were trying to persuade *me*. 'Madame Viret is a very famous person, you know. I hope you realize, Veronica, what a great honour she is doing you? You're a very lucky girl!'

I opened my mouth to say that of *course* Madame was a

famous person, and that of *course* it was an honour for her even to speak to me, let alone go to all that trouble for me. Then I closed it again, realizing that I couldn't ever make Aunt June understand what I felt. I don't believe she'd even taken it in that I'd been Madame's pupil for two whole years!

'Well, as I say, Madame Viret very kindly said she would arrange for your audition, and she will let us know when it is to take place,' Aunt June was saying. 'Of course you'll be going to London almost immediately. We shall just have to pay your school fees for the term you aren't there. A great pity!'

I felt like saying that if only Aunt June had listened to me in the first place, all this would never have happened. But I didn't. I felt that it would have sounded terribly ungrateful, and after all I *was* grateful. Aunt June had done what she considered to be her duty – had taken me in, and looked after me. She had been kind to me in her own way. I had been happy at Bracken Hall, knowing Sebastian and Caroline, learning to ride, and everything. I felt quite glad that I'd be coming back again in the holidays.

'It appears that your School Certificate won't be entirely wasted,' went on Aunt June. 'Madame Viret assured me that they like educated girls at the Sadler's Wells School. The modern idea, I suppose! Quite the contrary to what I imagined. In fact, you'll still go on with your studies – French, art, English literature, biology, history, and things like that – although, being over fifteen, you'll naturally be in the Senior School.'

She went on telling me all the things I already knew. As a matter of fact, there wasn't much I *didn't* know about the Wells!

Chapter 8

Catastrophe!

A week after Lady Blantosh's Bring and Buy Sale, Aunt June got a typewritten letter from the secretary of the Sadler's Wells School of Ballet saying that my audition was to be on the following Friday. It appeared that Madame had called to see Miss Martin in Newcastle on her way back to London, and between them they had fixed things up.

My thoughts were in a positive whirl, and by the time Thursday came, I was so excited I could neither eat nor sleep. Aunt June had booked a first-class sleeper for me from Newcastle to King's Cross, and I was to be put in special care of the sleeping-car attendant, who in his turn was to get me a porter at the other end of my journey. The porter would get me a taxi, and I was to go straight to Mrs Crapper and stay there until it was time for my audition at twelve o'clock. My ticket had already been bought and was reposing in the little drawer of my dressing-table. Perkins was to take me to the station in the car to catch the night train, which went at ten thirty-five. It was all very simple.

All very simple... How is it that it's always the simple things that turn out to be the most difficult, whereas, when you see breakers ahead, the sea is sure to turn out to be as calm as a millpond?

The Thursday morning dawned grey and misty. Aunt June was going to visit friends at Horchester, ten miles away. She took Perkins with her because of the mist, and promised she'd be back by nine o'clock at the latest so that there'd be plenty of time for Perkins to take me to the station. I was to be all ready to go, she said.

For the umpteenth time I checked over my dancing things – pink tights, black tunic, jock-belt, a pair of blocked and a pair of unblocked canvas practice shoes, a pair of my whitest socks, hairband, hairnet, not to mention plenty of hairgrips. I had washed the tights to make them fit without a wrinkle, as well as for cleanliness, and I'd ironed out the tunic, although I knew I should have to do it again at the other end. It wouldn't be exactly creaseless after it had spent the night in my suitcase! For the umpteenth time I tested the ribbons on my ballet shoes to make sure they were secure, and felt the blocks of my point shoes to see that they were hard enough. Lastly, I put into the case unimportant things like my nightie, toothbrush and my brush and comb – just in case I forgot them in the excitement of departure.

Then, on the top of everything, I carefully placed a small parcel wrapped in tissue paper. My mascot! Madame's shoes. Yes, they'd come back from the cleaners that very morning, and they were as good as new. At least, they were quite clean, though Messrs Britelite and Sons carefully explained in a polite little note they'd enclosed in the package that *they* weren't responsible for the worn patches. No, indeed – Covent Garden was responsible for them!

Well, after all this, there was nothing to do but wait as patiently as I could for Aunt June to return.

And all the time the mist grew thicker and thicker . . .

'I say,' Caroline said, as we came in from the stables at seven o'clock to wash our hands for supper, 'this mist is awful, isn't it? That's the worst of living on the edge of the moors; it comes down from the fells. I do hope—'

She stopped, and a pang of fright shot through me.

'Do hope what?'

'I was going to say I do hope Mummy leaves the Chiswicks

in plenty of time. It'll take Perkins ages to get back.'

I didn't say anything. I was quite sick with fear at the awful thought of missing that train. Surely, surely Fate wouldn't be so unkind as to dash the cup from my lips before I could drink!

At eight o'clock the telephone rang. I dashed to answer it before anyone else could get there. I knew quite certainly that it was about me, and I wanted to hear the worst. When I heard Aunt June's voice at the other end of the wire, I knew that it was indeed the worst!

'Oh, it's you, Veronica,' said the voice, sounding quite cheerful, and not a bit as if my whole future were at stake, 'I'm sorry, dear, about this frightful mist. I'm afraid it's quite impossible for me to get back tonight. Perkins won't risk it – the visibility here is practically nil.'

'But, Aunt June,' I wailed. 'My audition – my audition is tomorrow morning! Have you forgotten? I must – I simply *must* catch the train to London.'

'I'm afraid it's quite impossible, dear,' said the calm voice at the other end. 'We'll arrange another interview for you. It will be quite easy, I'm sure, when we explain. You see, Perkins—'

I put down the receiver, cutting off Aunt June and her maddening voice. 'Arrange another audition for me' – you didn't arrange auditions at a famous school like Sadler's Wells just like that! You were granted an audition, and you turned up for it, by hook or by crook, whether you had a streaming cold, or a splitting headache, whether there was a bus strike and you had to walk, or a pea-soup fog, or – or anything. You let *nothing* stop you! Why – *why* couldn't Aunt June understand? As for Perkins not daring to drive in the mist – I knew quite well that it wasn't Perkins who was afraid but Aunt June . . .

'What's the matter, Veronica?' said Caroline's anxious

voice from behind me. 'Is anything wrong?'

'Wrong?' I repeated. 'It's finished! My career's finished!'

'You mean?—'

'Aunt June can't get back tonight because of the mist,' I said. Then I added bitterly: 'It just doesn't dawn on her that my whole career is at stake.'

'I'm sure she realizes, Veronica,' Caroline put in gently, sticking up for her mother as she sometimes did most unexpectedly. 'It really is frightful outside, you know. I don't think *anyone* could possibly drive in it.'

I dashed away to hide my tears, leaving Caroline looking after me with a worried expression on her face, and Fiona smiling her hateful, knowing smile. I knew that Fiona was pleased that all my hopes were being crushed.

'I must, I *must* do something!' I said to myself. 'What can I do? Oh, God – *please* tell me what to do!'

Then suddenly I had an idea. I expect some people would say God had nothing to do with it – that God was far too busy to bother about a little thing like my dancing, but I was sure in my own mind that my idea was Heaven-sent, and that God was telling me what to do.

I tumbled my things out of my suitcase on to the floor, dashed into the schoolroom and pulled a rucksack from the bottom of the toy cupboard, where now book and tennis rackets and suchlike were kept, dashed back with it to my bedroom and hastily began to repack my things in it. I didn't bother about my nightie and toothbrush, this time, but squeezed in the dancing things as best I could, ending with Madame's shoes. Then, like a shadow, I slipped down the back stairs and out to the stables.

I daren't switch on the electric light for fear someone saw it and began asking questions, so I had to saddle up Arab by the light of my flashlamp. It was much harder than you'd think, but I managed it at last, and led the pony out into the stable yard. I went on leading him, so as to make as little noise as possible. I don't think I need have worried, really – the mist muffled his hooves as effectively as a blanket.

When we reached the long drive, I thought the mist didn't seem to be quite so thick, the reason for which I learned later on. At last I judged it safe to mount, and I did so, my rucksack bulging to bursting-point on my back. It was quite dark, though it was only half past eight and shouldn't have been for a long time yet, but this, I supposed, was owing to the mist.

As I reached the lodge gates, I wondered what Sebastian was doing – we hadn't seen him since the morning. And then, just as I drew level with the cottage, a voice said: 'Halt! Your money or your life! This is Daredevil Dick of the roving eye and the ready hand!'

I gave a gasp.

'Oh, Sebastian! You did give me a shock! I was just thinking about you.'

'Well, in that case I oughtn't to have given you a shock, ought I?' he laughed. 'I was just coming up to the Hall to see what had happened about this mist. I imagined they'd have got you into town ages ago. And by the way. "where are you going to my pretty maid" at this time of night, if you don't mind my asking?'

My thoughts flashed back to a day, more than a year ago now – a morning in July when I'd been perched on the top of this very gate, and Sebastian's voice had asked almost the same question. I gave the same answer now. I said: 'I'm running away. I am really! I'm not joking. You see . . .'

Then out it all came. Aunt June's visit to Horchester; the mist; my audition. Of course, Sebastian knew all about that.

'So you see, I ended, 'I've just *got* to go – mist or no mist.'

'But, Veronica, you *can't* go,' Sebastian said, his voice sounding anxious and tense. 'You couldn't possibly, you know. You'd never get there in time, anyway.'

'Of course I know I can't catch *that* train,' I argued. 'But there'll be another one – a mail train or a milk train early in the morning. There are trains to London all the time. There must be one; there *must*! My audition isn't till twelve. I might just get there. Anyway, I'm going to have a jolly good try – they say you can do anything if you really make up your mind to it.' I kicked Arab sharply, and we shot off into the mist. Fortunately the gates had been left open for Aunt June and Perkins. I felt pretty sure Sebastian wouldn't have opened them for me!

'Veronica!' came Sebastian's voice out of the mist. 'Don't be an idiot – you don't know what you're taking on – honestly you don't. The mist is nothing here to what it'll be when you get away from the trees. It's never so thick where there are trees. There are no buses, you know. This isn't a market day—'

'You said that a year ago, I remember!' I said with an excited laugh. 'Well, I shall *ride* to Newcastle if necessary. I don't care! I shall get there somehow. Goodbye!'

But I had reckoned without the mist. As Sebastian had said, the moment Arab and I left the trees it closed round us like muffling folds of cottonwool. A figure loomed up beside us and caught hold of Arab's bridle. Sebastian again! I might have known he wouldn't be so easily shaken off.

'Veronica – you've *got* to stop. I order you to stop!'

'You take your hand away from my bridle, or I'll – I'll ...' I raised my crop threateningly, though I didn't really mean to strike him with it.

Then suddenly Sebastian let go. With a gasp of relief, and not a little of astonishment, I saw him vanish into the mist, and I was once more alone. I say 'with relief' but really it was with rather mixed feelings that I saw him go – he seemed to be my last friend in a nightmare world. But I set my teeth and determined not to give in. I *must* get there somehow, I told

171

myself – mist or no mist. The audition – Sadler's Wells – my beloved dancing career ... Thoughts raced round in my head as I urged Arab onwards.

Strange noises came from all round me. Then I realized that they were only the sounds of the countryside – sounds you don't notice in broad daylight with the sun shining – a cow coughing, or blowing down its nose on the far side of the hedge; an owl screeching; the metallic whirr of a grouse rising in alarm out of a nearby thicket. It was terribly eerie and queer. My heart began to beat quickly and I wished that Sebastian hadn't given in like that and gone away. It would have been a comfort to have had his company, even if he *had* argued all the time.

Then, out of the mist, came a familiar sound behind me – the sound of a horse trotting.

A thrill of fright went through me. I was being pursued! I thought of all the people Sebastian might have told about me running away. His father, Uncle Adrian; then I remembered Sebastian saying that he was away. Uncle John – but he'd rung up to say he'd be staying in town for the night, as he always did if there was a mist. Trixie – she certainly couldn't ride on horseback. Pilks, Dickson. Neither could they – certainly not in a mist like this! It could only be Sebastian himself. Perhaps he thought he had more chance of stopping me when he was mounted. Well, he'd see! I drew in to the side of the road and waited for the rider to come up with me – I knew by the way he was trotting that I hadn't the ghost of a chance of escaping by speed, not being able to do more than a very slow walk myself.

'That you, Veronica?' came Sebastian's voice after a few minutes. 'I thought you couldn't have got far.'

'If you think you're going to stop me ...' I began desperately. 'If you think—'

'Stop being melodramatic, my dear cousin-sort-of,' said

Sebastian in his usual bantering tones, 'and let's get going! We'll have to step on the gas – and how! – if you mean to catch your milk train – if there *is* a milk train.'

'You don't mean that you're coming with me?' I said with a thrill of joy and hope.

'I certainly *do* mean it,' said Sebastian. 'Nothing else to be done as far as I can see – or rather I should say *feel*. More accurate! I always know when I'm beaten, and I could tell by the sound of your voice just now that nothing short of prison bars would stop you from venturing into the wild. Well, as I haven't any prison bars handy, the only thing to do is to come along with you myself and see you don't exceed the speed limit! I said to myself: "The girl's quite determined – obvious she can't go by herself. Get lost for one thing; take the wrong turning; get run over most likely. Anyway, certainly wouldn't get anywhere – not in this mist, being a Cockney brat." So I had to do the Boy Scout stunt. Can't let a fellow *artiste* down, if you see what I mean. This is my good deed for today!'

'Sebastian, you're a *brick*!' I said, trying not to burst out crying for joy and relief. 'As you say, "let's get going".'

Chapter 9

Journey Through the Mist

To be caught in a mist at night on a moorland road in Northumberland doesn't sound so dreadful, but you try it! I was quite hardened to the London fogs when you could only see a few inches in front of your nose, but in London you were at least among other people. There were lighted shops on all sides to cheer you, even if you *could* only see them dimly, as if through smoked glass. There were kindly policemen at crossings and corners, doing all they could to help you; there was noise, and bustle, and the friendly Underground where you could nearly forget about the fog outside. But here, on this lonely road, with the unseen hills wrapped in cloud all around you, the silence was intense. The only sounds that broke it were the occasional prattle of a moorland stream as it tumbled over its stony bed, or the plaintive cry of a peewit or a curlew.

The moorland road was unfenced and at first I'd been terrified for fear my pony strayed off the path on to the endless open moor that stretched away on every side. But I found that Sebastian knew exactly what to do about that – he just let Warrior have his head and Warrior kept to the road all right. He hadn't been born and bred on the Northumbrian moors for nothing! I found that Arab was just as wise. Our only worry was knowing which way to go when we came to a fork, or a crossroads. Fortunately Sebastian had brought his torch, which saved the situation. Although several times he had to climb the signposts to get near enough to flash the light on to the names we did at least know we were going in the right direction.

'It's a good thing you brought that torch, Sebastian,' I said, after one of our many stops. 'I had one too, but I left it in the stable. I never thought of bringing it with me.'

'No, I rather guessed you wouldn't,' said Sebastian with laughter in his voice. 'All you would think of bringing would be a pair of ballet shoes and some tights! Not much use for a night out in the mist!'

I blushed guiltily in the dark, when I remembered how carefully I had packed Madame's precious shoes into my rucksack, not bothering to bring a brush and comb, or even a nightie! Sebastian came perilously near the truth!

'I wonder what they thought when they found I'd gone?' I said suddenly. 'Trixie, and Caroline, and all of them. Oh, Sebastian – I quite forgot to leave a note to explain! How dreadful of me! Do you think they'll be awfully worried?'

'Oh, no – shouldn't think so,' said Sebastian. 'I expect they'll say: "Oh, well – that's the end of her", shut the door and go to bed. "No need to worry; people disappear every day."' Then I think he sensed how upset I really was at what I had done – or rather what I had *not* done, for his teasing tone changed and he said seriously: 'It's OK, Veronica! I left a letter to my father telling him what had happened. He'll get it when he comes back from the village. I think he'll agree that it was the only thing to do – sensible chap, my father! By the way—' He stopped suddenly.

'Yes – what?'

'Well, you remember when we were discussing our Matric results the other day?'

'Yes, what about it?'

'Well, you remember when Fiona said something about me *needing* to do well because of my career. She said: "You'll have to be pretty clever if you're going to be a barrister." And I said: "Yes – *if* I'm going to be a barrister."'

'Yes,' I said. 'I remember.'

'The fact is,' went on Sebastian, the excitement in his voice making it wobble a little, 'the fact is, Veronica, it's definitely fixed, and I'm *not* going in for Law. I had it out with my father the other day, and I'm going to make Music my career. You're the very first person to know.'

'Oh, Sebastian, I'm so glad!' I exclaimed. 'I know what it's like to want to do something most awfully and have everyone against you.'

'When all came to all,' continued Sebastian, 'Father said he'd half suspected the truth. He said that no one could remain totally oblivious of the fact that my heart was in the piano, judging by the number of hours I spend sitting at it! I *have* practised rather a lot these hols,' he added apologetically. 'In fact I've done nothing else – except ride with you lot now and then. Well, my father agreed that it was no earthly good my taking up Law as a profession if my heart was set on other things, so I'm to try for a scholarship to the Royal College of Music next year. He really was most awfully decent about it – he's an understanding chap is my father. If I get the scholarship I'm coming to London to study, so you'll be able to come to the Albert Hall with me, and I'll go to Covent Garden with you, what!'

After this there was silence between us for a long time. We were each far too deep in our own thoughts to talk. It was a good thing our thoughts were blissful, because the outlook was anything but cheerful. 'Outlook' is quite the wrong word, really, because we couldn't see anything at all now – not even the ditches at the sides of the road. If it hadn't been for the wonderful sixth sense of our ponies we'd have been blundering into them at every step. The mist seemed to get thicker and thicker, and we got colder and colder.

'This is the top of the road over Cushat's Crag, you know,' said Sebastian, breaking the long silence. 'I shouldn't be surprised if the mist isn't at its worst here. It usually is. If the mist is rolling off the hills, as it is tonight, and not rising off the low ground – well, you're right in the middle of the clouds up here. When we get over the top and go down the other side it may thin out a bit.'

'How many miles have we come?' I asked. 'We seem to have been riding for hours and hours.'

'About ten miles,' said Sebastian. Then he flashed his torch on to his wristwatch. 'It's half past eleven, so it's taken us two hours. We have another twenty miles to go to get to Newcastle. When we get on to the Military Road that runs along the Roman Wall, we might come across a garage. There's one at the crossroads – at least I *think* it's a garage, but it may only be a filling station. We might knock them up and get a taxi – at least we might if the mist lifts a bit. I'm pretty sure they wouldn't turn out in this, no matter what we offered them. We'll have to get a lift somehow, you know, and hang the expense! You won't be fit for anything tomorrow after this.'

'Oh, yes I shall,' I said, trying to stop my teeth chattering. 'B-ballet dancers are pretty t-tough.'

'Hullo! What's this?' exclaimed Sebastian, reining in Warrior. 'Golly! A covered-in bus stop. What a find! Let's stop here and rest the ponies for a bit, shall we?'

We tethered the ponies to an iron railing that stretched away into the mist on either side of the tiny shelter, and sank down thankfully on the hard wooden seat inside. Once more Sebastian flashed on his torch, and I saw by its light that he had swung round his rucksack and was taking something out of it – a Thermos flask and a packet of sandwiches.

'I told you once before that I always carry my own canteen about with me, didn't I?' he said. 'Brainwave, what! It was a good thing Bella had just made the coffee and stood it on the stove to keep hot. I'd like to have been there when she found it gone. She wouldn't even be able to blame the cat – not with

177

hot coffee! I'm afraid I made a bad job of the sandwiches. Hadn't much time, you see, and I couldn't find anything to go in them, except cheese.'

'It tastes like caviare!' I laughed. 'I mean, just as wonderful.'

'I hope not!' Sebastian said solemnly. 'Personally I loathe caviare. Filthy stuff!'

'Oh, I love it,' I said. 'Jonathan always had it when he sold a picture and threw a party!'

'It's a good thing we don't all like the same things,' pronounced Sebastian. 'I'll have the ice-cream, and you can have the caviare.'

'Oh, but I like ice-cream, too!'

'Well, what *don't* you like?'

I thought long and deeply. Finally I said: 'Tripe.'

'Don't like it either,' laughed Sebastian. 'So what?'

'Deadlock, I'm afraid,' I said. 'I seem to be frightfully easy to please. I like simply everything. Oh, no – I've just thought of something I simply *loathe* – caraway seeds!'

'Love 'em!' declared Sebastian. 'So the situation is saved at the eleventh hour. You can have my caviare, and I'll have your caraway seeds!'

We stayed quite a long time in the shelter so as to give the ponies a good rest – and ourselves too. When at last we decided it was time to move, it was twelve o'clock.

'The witching hour!' exclaimed Sebastian as we rode off. 'Now is the time for hobgoblins, witches, earthbound spirits, and every sort of uncanny thing to be abroad!'

'Ugh!' I said. 'Don't! You make me feel creepy! The mist is uncanny enough – without your ghostly et ceteras!'

For ages and ages we rode onwards, and the silence between us grew longer as we grew more and more weary. Arab was beginning to stumble and Warrior's trot had lost its springy

178

sound. We walked the ponies quite a lot of the time.

'I wonder where we are now?' I said, with a sigh of utter weariness. 'It seems hours and hours since we left that bus stop.'

'It is,' answered Sebastian. 'Two, anyway... Gosh! D'you see what's happened? The mist is thinning. I can see that signpost clearly. We're coming to the crossroads I told you about. Now for our garage!'

But alas! The garage proved to be a mere filling station as Sebastian had feared. It was as black and dead-looking as the dodo.

'The chappie probably lives miles away,' Sebastian said. 'It's no use our trying to ferret him out, because we don't know in which direction the nearest village is. Of course we might go back and try Simonburn—'

'Oh, let's *not*,' I said. 'Simonburn is the other way to Newcastle, isn't it? I don't want to go back – I want to go *on*!'

We went on. We passed an AA box, with a telephone inside, but alas! it was no use to us as we hadn't a key.

'A friend of mine lives somewhere about here,' said Sebastian after a bit. 'Or rather his father does. His name is Dillon – Jack Dillon – and they have a farm hereabouts. Ah, I thought so! Here it is – Hunter's Copse.' He stopped in the middle of the road and flashed his torch so that I could read the name on the gate.

'Look out!' I yelled. 'There's something coming!' It was a car, judging by the two pale lights gleaming through the fog. To my surprise Sebastian flung himself off Warrior's back, and leapt into the middle of the road, waving his arms wildly and yelling at the top of his voice.

'Stop! Stop! Hi – wait a minute!'

Fortunately the driver had good eyesight and was going at a snail's pace. He stopped at once, let down the window of the car and yelled back: 'What's that? You in any trouble?'

'You've said it!' yelled back Sebastian. 'Half a mo' and we'll tell you about it. You can help us a lot if you will. Filthy night, isn't it?'

'Filthy?' said the man in the car. 'I could find a better name for it than that! Are you two youngsters alone?'

'Yes,' said Sebastian. 'That is, we've got our ponies, of course. You see ...' There, on that foggy and deserted road in the wilds of Northumberland, with a bit of help from me, he told our story – all about the Bring and Buy Sale, Madame, my audition at Sadler's Wells, and finally the last awful catastrophe – Aunt June and the mist. I expect it sounded a bit fantastic. Anyway, when we'd finished, the man whistled and said in an awestruck voice: 'My holy godfathers! And you two have ridden on a couple of ponies all the way from Bracken to here, and you are prepared to do another twenty miles or so to Newcastle, in order to catch a hypothetical train to London. My sainted aunt!'

'We *did* hope you would give us a lift, sir,' said Sebastian hopefully.

'A lift?' said the man. 'I should just say I could! But look here – I can get you two in the back all right but how about the animals? I doubt if they'd go in the boot! Do we tow them, or what? No doubt you have ideas! You don't seem lacking in ingenuity!'

'I have a friend who lives at this farm,' Sebastian explained, waving in the direction of the gateway on our right. 'We could leave the ponies here and I could collect them tomorrow morning. The mist'll have cleared off by then, and I could ride them back all right – I mean ride one and lead the other.'

'But, Sebastian,' I expostulated, 'won't your friend object to being knocked up at two o'clock in the morning?'

Sebastian laughed shortly.

'I should just say he would! We needn't disturb him,

though. As a matter of fact the farm is a couple of miles off the road, but I happen to know that this field is pasture' – he flashed his torch on to the short grass inside the gate to reassure me – 'and the animals will be quite OK. I'll be back to collect them before he even knows they're there!'

'Well, that's an idea, certainly,' said the man in the car. 'You two do the doings, and I'll have a smoke meantime. The night's young! I ought to have been in Newcastle before midnight, but now it's of no account when I get there. May as well be hung for a sheep as a lamb!'

He flicked open his lighter, and I saw his eyes. They re-assured me, being all crinkly round the edges, as if he laughed a lot. I breathed a sigh of relief. Being town bred, I felt it was a bit risky to go making friends with strangers in the middle of a moor at two o'clock in the morning!

As I fondled Arab's warm, silky neck before setting him free, I suddenly realized that I was saying a long goodbye to my pony. If I was accepted as a pupil of the Wells School I shouldn't be coming back here until the holidays, and who knew what might happen to Arabesque? Aunt June would most probably send him back to his owner at Merlingford, and I would see him no more. A tear stole down my nose at the thought of it.

'Come on! What are you waiting for?' said Sebastian's voice at my elbow. 'We're all ready, aren't we? I'll dump the tack in this spinney – I certainly don't feel like taking it with us to Newcastle – I should have to cart it all the way back tomorrow. Just shine the light, will you?'

I held the torch whilst Sebastian climbed the railings into a little copse that lay between the field and the road on one side of the gate. He pushed the saddles and bridles under a thick tangle of blackberry bushes, and piled bracken on top of them.

'Nobody will know they're there,' he declared when he had finished. 'Only hope it doesn't rain really hard, that's all!'

We went back to the car and got inside. Never had a car felt so warm and luxurious as that old and battered Ford Eight – not even Aunt June's palatial Rolls! We sank down on the imitation leather cushions with a sigh of thankfulness, feeling that the worst of our long trek was over.

We got to Newcastle Central Station at exactly half past four, the mist having thinned considerably as we drove eastwards. We learned that there was a train to London at a quarter to six, so Sebastian led the way to the one and only buffet which was open all night, and procured two large, thick cups of steaming hot coffee and a plate of doorstep sandwiches. Ordinarily we might have turned up our noses at them, but after our ordeal we were only too thankful to get a hot drink and something to eat. When we had finished, we went to the general waiting-room. There were several people sitting or lying on the seats and quite a few slumped over the centre table, fast asleep, their heads on their arms. Sebastian found the woman who was in charge of the place, and tipped her a shilling to wake us up in time for the London train. Then we lay down on an empty bench, our heads at opposite ends like a couple of sardines. Sebastian had taken off his coat and he covered us both with it. We used our rucksacks for pillows because the bench was made of wood and was pretty hard to lie on. I must add that I removed my point shoes (and Madame's) from the rucksack before I lay on it for fear I squashed them!

'Goodnight, Veronica,' Sebastian said with a yawn. 'We managed it OK, didn't we?'

'Oh, Sebastian,' I said, half to myself. 'You *are* sweet!'

'What's that?' asked Sebastian sleepily.

'Oh, nothing,' I answered, knowing by past experience that under no circumstances must you call a boy 'sweet'! 'Goodnight!'

* * *

Fortunately the train started from Newcastle, so it was punctual. There were no sleepers on it, even if I had the necessary cash, which I hadn't, but Sebastian managed to hire me a rug and a pillow. How he did it I don't know, but I was full of gratitude and admiration. I couldn't help thinking of the time when I had held the view that people who lived in Northumberland were next door to savages. Sebastian knew a great deal more about travelling than I did – there was no denying the fact.

'Mind you get a taxi straight to the school,' he said as the guard began slamming carriage doors. 'And don't forget the address – 45 Colet Gardens, Baron's Court.'

'As if I should!' I laughed. 'Why, it's written on my heart!'

'So long, Veronica!' he yelled, as the train began to slide away from the platform. 'Good luck!'

'Goodbye!' I yelled back. 'And thank you for everything!'

His face swam in a mist before my eyes, and I realized that I was no longer laughing – I was crying! It wasn't only leaving Sebastian behind that made me cry, but all the other things too – Arabesque, the moors, Caroline, Bracken Hall itself. I realized, too late, that I hadn't even said a proper goodbye to them.

As the train got up speed, I lay down on the seat and tried to sleep, but the carriage wheels seemed as if they were turning in my head, and the melody they played was the *Holberg Suite*. My heart had a queer feeling – as if someone was slowly squeezing it – a feeling I hadn't had for a very long time; in fact, not since that journey north more than a year ago. How queer, I thought, that on that occasion I had been homesick for the noisy Underground and all the sounds and sights of London. Now my heart was aching for the moors and woods of Northumberland!

The *Holberg Suite* changed to the Dance of the Sugar Plum Fairy, then to *Les Sylphides*, and finally the whirring of the wheels merged into the unearthly music of Tchaikovsky's *Swan Lake*. I slept at last.

Chapter 10

Sadler's Wells at Last

The train was only a quarter of an hour late. I learned from some well-informed passengers that the fog had lifted as soon as we had left Darlington behind, and the train had made up time on the southern part of the journey. It was half past eleven when I dashed through the barrier at King's Cross and made for the taxi rank. There was a touch on my arm.

'Veronica!'

I turned in surprise; then gave a gasp of joy. There in front of me was a well-known figure, towering above the other passengers – a young man with a shock of unruly black hair, and a little black beard.

'Jonathan! Whatever are you doing here?'

'It looks as if I'm meeting *you*!' he laughed.

'But how did you—' I began.

'Look,' said Jonathan, taking my arm and hurrying me along. 'D'you mind if we leave the explanations until we're in the taxi – we'll have to get moving, you know, if we're to get to Baron's Court by twelve o'clock. And I expect you'll need a few spare minutes to titivate—' He whirled me along and into the taxi.

'Five minutes will do!' I laughed, as I sank on to the seat. 'Oh, Jonathan, it *is* good to see you! I was feeling dreadfully homesick, but now it's as though I've come home instead! But please, will you explain how you knew I was on that train. I didn't know I was going to be on it myself until half past five this morning.'

'Just a moment,' said Jonathan. 'Mrs Crapper, the dear old soul, said I was to give you this, and to be sure you drank it' – he pulled a Thermos flask out of his pocket. 'She said she was sure you wouldn't have had any breakfast. Have you?'

'Well, no – I haven't,' I confessed.

'Get on with these then,' went on Jonathan, producing a packet of sandwiches out of the other pocket. 'You've only a few minutes. Well, now for the explanation. At a most un-civilized hour in the morning – six-thirty to be exact – I was roused from my downy pillow by a long-distance telephone call. It was from a friend of yours way up north – a young man, I guessed, from the voice.'

'Sebastian!' I gasped, pausing with a sandwich halfway to my mouth. 'He isn't a young man; he's a boy, and my cousin. At least a sort of a cousin. But how did he find your number? I never told it to him – in fact I don't know it myself. At least I did, but I've forgotten it.'

'Well, I'm as much in the dark there as you are!' laughed Jonathan. 'All I can suggest is that he knew my address and badgered the exchange until they looked up my number.'

'Oh, he'd do that all right!' I exclaimed. 'Trust Sebastian!'

'Anyway, he got me all right,' went on Jonathan. 'And he told me the tale, and here I am, half asleep through being robbed of my beauty sleep, but willing! And by the way, Veronica – congratulations!'

'Keep them till afterwards!' I said, finishing off the coffee. 'They may think I'm frightful and turn me away. Gosh! Here we are. Oh, Jonathan – I feel *awful*!'

'Keep your pecker up!' said Jonathan. 'I'll be waiting for you with the taxi at the corner. Best of luck!'

At exactly twelve o'clock I walked into the studio where I'd been told my audition would take place. My hair was neatly fastened in the net, my tights pulled up, and the creases in my tunic smoothed out as much as possible. I had a queer feeling in my inside, like when you dive off the high springboard at the swimming baths for the first time, and my legs felt as if they belonged to somebody else. My hour had come – the hour I had thought of, and dreamed of for so long. I could hardly believe it.

The audition wasn't really so terrifying after all. Only a pretty fair-haired lady and a quiet gentleman with sad, dark eyes that looked as if they saw through you, and far beyond you, and yet made you feel at home just the same. I learned afterwards that usually part of the audition takes place in an ordinary class, but Madame had managed to get me one all to myself because the school hadn't yet started after the holidays.

While I was doing some *grands-jetés* the door of the studio opened and another gentleman looked in. He watched me for a moment, and then said: 'Come! You can spring higher than that! Try again!'

I was very tired, but he didn't know that, of course, and I certainly wasn't going to tell him, because that would have looked like making excuses for myself. I made up my mind to jump higher than I had ever done before – somehow he made me want to do it.

'Good!' he said approvingly. 'I knew you could! Your elevation is excellent. You've got a nice line, too.'

Then suddenly I recognized him. He was the temperamental ballet master I had watched the day I'd gatecrashed. And here he was being quite friendly! With a smile and a nod he shut the door again, and went away.

When I had done all they asked, the lady told me to take off my socks. She examined my feet most carefully, asking me all sorts of questions as to whether I had ever had any trouble with my feet, whether they ever ached, whether I had ever sprained either of my ankles, all of which I answered truthfully in the negative. Finally she murmured: 'Very nice!' told me I could put on my socks again, and go.

'Please – *please*!' I begged. 'Is it all right? Can I come? Of course I expect it's all against the rules, but couldn't you – couldn't you just tell me if I can come?'

The gentleman looked at the lady and they both smiled.

'Well,' said the gentleman, 'it *is* a little – shall we say unusual, but I think we can put you out of your misery. If you really think you'll be happy here, and don't mind hard work, well, yes – you shall come.'

'Oh, *thank* you!' I said. 'I know I shall be happy. When your dream comes true, you're bound to be happy, aren't you? And as for work – I'll – I'll work my fingers to the bone ...' I stopped suddenly, realizing that this was rather a queer way to put it when one was referring to ballet! 'I mean, I'll do the very best I can if you'll let me work here.'

'That is all that is necessary,' said the lady, writing something in a book. 'And now I expect you'll want to be going? The secretary will write to your aunt about times and so on. Term begins on Monday and you'll be in the Junior class.' Then she looked at me rather hard, and added: 'You look tired, dear. Were you very excited about your audition?'

'Yes,' I said, 'but not as excited as I would have been if it hadn't been for missing the train last night.' Then out it all came – Aunt June's visit, my flight from Bracken Hall, and my encounter with Sebastian. As I talked, I realized how queer it must all sound, here in civilized London, with the Underground, and the buses, not to mention taxis at every street corner, all taking you wherever you wanted to go at a moment's notice.

'And then the car came along,' I finished, 'and that was the end of our adventure – except that Sebastian will have to collect the ponies this morning and ride them all that way back – twenty miles, at least.'

'A real friend in need – that young man!' said the quiet gentleman. Then he murmured something to the lady about the grit and tenacity of these North Country children. 'And, after all, it's what we need,' he added. 'That, along with other qualities.'

'Oh, but it was Sebastian who was tenacious,' I said quickly. 'I'd never have managed it if it hadn't been for him. You don't *know* how marvellous he was!'

'I think these was grit on both sides,' declared the gentleman with a smile. 'I'm glad to see that you don't easily give up, my dear, when you make up your mind to do a thing.'

And that was the end of my audition. As I left the building, I looked back and gave a sigh of happiness:

45 Colet Gardens – Sadler's Wells School of Ballet.

My dream had come true!

Also by Lorna Hill
Veronica at the Wells 40p

Veronica is now at the Sadler's Wells Ballet School and her first
days are exciting, even a little frightening, for not everyone welcomes
the talented newcomer. When she is fifteen, Veronica has the most
wonderful Christmas present – her first part at Covent Garden.

No Castanets at the Wells 40p

This book in the Wells series is about Caroline Scott, Veronica
Weston's cousin, who suddenly decides to slim and take ballet
seriously. She succeeds in passing her audition and meets many
favourite characters from earlier stories.

Masquerade at the Wells 40p

Jane and Mariella Foster were two cousins with everything and
nothing in common – Mariella, daughter of a prima-ballerina,
loved the horses and dogs in the outdoor life that Jane was forced
to lead, while Jane longed for the ballet lessons which Mariella
ridiculed. Read what happens when a daring deception is thought
up and Jane takes Mariella's place at an audition for the Sadler's
Wells Ballet School.

Honor Arundel
The High House 40p

When her mother and father are killed in a car crash, thirteen-year-old Emma goes to live with her aunt in Edinburgh. Aunt Patsy is a freelance designer and is always waiting for the next cheque to arrive. To begin with, Emma finds it difficult to adjust to the new way of life – but soon she begins to enjoy it.

Emma's Island 40p

Emma is now living on the island of Stranday, and has to cope with all sorts of practical and emotional problems. Then the summer brings Alastair, a student from Glasgow, and Emma falls in love for the very first time.

Emma in Love 40p

Back in Edinburgh again, Emma is now keeping house for her student brother and studying hard at school, as well as continuing her exciting friendship with Alastair.

Enid Blyton

Now you can read the complete series of stories about the four children Jack, Lucy-Ann, Philip and Dinah and their parrot Kiki. They can never go anywhere, however ordinary, without having a thrilling and exciting adventure.